Tuscan Dream

ISBN: 1-4776-2139-3
ISBN-13: 9781477621394

Tuscan Dream

A novel

Narendra Simone

"Deliverance? Where is this deliverance to be found? Our master himself has joyfully taken upon him the bonds of creation; he is bound with us all forever."

Gitanjali
Rabindranath Tagore

Praise for Narendra's Books:

"Reading *Desert Song* is what I imagine a few evenings to be like of listening to a master story teller take us through the descent of Beowulf. Medieval in its proportions, gruesome in its verity, raw in its necessity, *Desert Song* exposes the sinister triangulations of politics, religion, and law in a world wrought with dark forces. Our hero, Matt Slater, witnesses unimaginable crimes in his desperate search for a lost child. Startling ironies erupt on each page as Simone's first thriller hurtles us through a journey both disturbing and authentic. Before you read any other book on the Taliban, read this book first."—Almeda Glenn Miller, author of *"Tiger Dreams"*

"In his riveting story, The Last Goodbye, Narendra Simone skillfully portrays the soul of a mother/son relationship in a culture that remains an enigma to so many of us."—Mike Sirota, author of *"Fire Dance"* and *"The Burning Ground"*.

"Right from the beginning I enjoyed Narendra's style...the picture was drawn and I stepped right into the set...he cleverly interweaves his characters and gives his reader intrigue and interest in learning the dangerous world of Arabia...Once I started reading it I could not wait to finish it."—Praveen Gupta, Published Author of 14 Books

Prologue

It was a dreary December day. A pigeon perched on Maria's windowsill, cooing its mindless melody. A slight chill in the air added to the misery of the damp day. And lying there awake, Maria felt dull and blackened, as if hate were corroding her body. She stayed in bed, exhausted. She couldn't remember another time in her life when she had loathed herself. But now, hate lodged in her throat, thick and ugly, making her feel diseased.

Maria tried to smile at the old priest she had known all her life, now softly knocking at her open bedroom door. With her strained smile she invited him to step inside. She tried to sit up but failed as a bolt of sharp pain shot through her; the growing cancer had sapped her strength and rendered her already frail body useless. Her face contorted in a grimace and her eyes apologized for her disheveled appearance.

The priest with a solemn face that expressed more care than customary, approached her bed, fluffed up her pillows, placed them against the headboard, and gently helped her up to rest against them. Almost breathless with the effort, she nodded to show her appreciation and her face bore a mixed expression of sadness and relief. Sadness because she felt the presence of death in her room as if waiting for an opportune time to snatch her soul from her cancer-ravaged, almost forty-year-old body, and relief because the priest was there to receive her confession. It was time.

"How are you, Padre?" she said in a voice that showed appreciation and gratitude for his visit. "I've ignored Him for a while, haven't I?"

"He has not forsaken you, my child," he replied in a soft voice, as if imparting a secret. "I know you have faith and you have been faithful to Him. He will receive you when the time comes and you mustn't be afraid, for His kingdom is beautiful." His words, though habitually comforting, carried the extra weight of sincerity as he gazed upon her with concerned eyes. Her eyes were moist as she listened to the comforting words, for she had not received kindness from anyone for a long time.

"Thank you, Padre," she murmured and held out her balled-up hands towards the priest as if raised in supplication. "I feel comforted now that you're here. It means a lot for you to visit me. To be honest with you, I'm not afraid of death; it is dying under these terrible circumstances that terrifies me." Suddenly a look of sadness covered her face like a dark cloud and she stared at nothing in particular. A silent moment passed. "I've seen such wickedness in my life. I cannot die like this, I must confess. I've secrets that must not go with me to my grave," she said in a low and wavering voice. Her eyes betrayed the tone of her voice with an edge of steel, indicating that she had reconciled her conflicting emotions and was ready for her last confession. "Would you," she faltered as if unaccustomed to such requests, but persevered, "would you help me, Father?"

"That I will. But you look so weak, are you in pain? Can I do something to make you more comfortable?" The priest tried to comfort her to make her imminent journey to the heavenly abode as painless as possible. He had known for a while from various sources within his congregation that her cancer has unabatedly spread as she refused to take medication or undergo treatment. Maria had accepted the cancer as a just punishment for her sins and had vowed not to interfere with the justice delivered by the hand of God; she was a devout Catholic.

A faint smile on Maria's face reappeared when she answered the priest, "Pain in my body only serves to soothe the agony in my heart. But you will pray for all this to be over soon, won't you, Father?"

The priest held in his hands her clenched fists and nodded his concurrence. At his touch her hands balled up even tighter and her body stiffened, as if the touch of the priest's hands had given her an electric shock. He drew his hands away from her and gazed at her with gentle eyes, assuring her of the Lord's help.

The light had begun to fade as growing darkness outside gradually swallowed the dusk light. The priest turned on the bedside light and immediately Maria's eyelids flickered to cut the sharp glare. He turned the light off. The priest walked over to the lamp, a solid, tall brass pole fitted with a large, faded yellow lampshade with matching fringe, and turned the light on.

The soft yellow-orange glow filled the room. The fringe of the lampshade quivered momentarily then gently settled back to its motionless state. The priest grasped the back of the wooden chair and watched Maria with raised eyebrows as she slowly nodded, gesturing for him to bring the chair closer to her bed. The priest moved the chair next to her bedside and sat down in the ornate walnut chair, cushioned with crushed maroon velvet.

For a moment Maria's mind drifted into the darkness of the past. Eclipsed between the diminishing light and rising darkness there exists a time called the twilight of love, synonymous with the space between love and hate that dwells in the hearts of those who question their life partners, the ones destiny bestowed on them. Their feelings, once charged with passion and surging desire, have moved on with the passing of time, but their hopes of redemption and reconciliation remain and they feel vacant and abandoned. How does one let go of such feelings when they are wrapped around one's soul like a parasite creeper around a tree trunk, sapping its life. She took a deep sigh filled with sadness and said, "Old sins cast long shadows."

"Whatever do you mean?" asked Padre.

"Some people have died," said Maria in a contemplative voice with a grimace on her face, "and some are alive and you, Padre, you deal with both. But what you may not know is that there are people neither alive nor dead."

"It is the Lord who receives them," he said and pushed his chair a little closer, gazing into her eyes, "and He forgives them all. Have you asked for forgiveness?"

Maria blankly stared at the ceiling and in a voice that reflected pain said, "I've repented and I have paid."

"It's not a matter of paying," the priest said in an empathetic tone as he touched the heavy metal cross around his neck and then smoothed his dalmatic down, tugged at its long sleeves, and added, "you can't buy forgiveness, it is free. But you have to ask for it. Have you asked for it?"

Maria looked at the priest and, with a faint smile, licked her dry lips. The priest picked up the glass by her bedside table and helped lift her head by slipping his arm under it. She took a small sip and blinked, indicating she'd had enough.

She let him replace the glass on the table and she continued, "And from whom do you suggest I should ask for forgiveness? Forgive me, Padre, but not from Him. I did not do anything wrong to Him except to give my utmost devotion. I want forgiveness from those to whom I did wrong. But they are not here, so where do you suggest I go now to receive this forgiveness?"

It was his turn to smile and he was not new to this game. He nodded gently and in a tone like a whisper he answered, "He listens from and for all. If you do your part, He will do His."

Her smile widened. "Okay. Well, I'm ready and I'm asking now."

"Then He is listening. Now," said the priest in a soothing tone, "what secrets are tormenting your soul? I'm here for you."

"I've done wrong, Father," she repeated and her face darkened with the memories of her past. "I've told terrible lies. I am afraid that my savior may not forgive me."

"The Lord forgives us all, Mary. You don't know the ways of the Lord."

"You don't know my lies."

Maria's hands remain clenched and she placed them on her chest as she stared vacantly at the large window. She wished it would rain. Maria loved rain. Her mind began to drift like a solo cloud being pushed by high winds drifting across a vast landscape. So many years had gone by, and in that old world her youth had been so convulsed and shattered that, as she looked back and tried to recapture the details of particular scenes, they dissolved like a few drops of rain in the distance. But it was not important to her anymore, only salvation was.

Maria shook her head to lift the fog in her mind. She remembered in particular the rainy day some ten years back when she was sitting at her favorite dormer window in this very bedroom after taking a walk with her sister to the Stazione Centrale located in Piazza Delia Stazione in Florence.

Book I
Ten Years Ago
Florence, Italy

Spring 1983
"Love purifies the heart like spring glorifies blossoms."

1

Maria wrapped her slender hands around the mug of steamy coffee with streamers of smoke steadily rising, enveloping her face in secrecy. She sat by the large dormer window on the third and top story located directly above the main entrance door at the street level of her house. Come rain or shine, Maria never closed the blue shutters of her dormer window and loved the breeze that always seemed to bring freshness during the day and coolness in the night. On the windowsill were two heavy blue ceramic pots in which she had planted fern, tropical in their form and so resilient to the frequent Florence rain.

She loved the soft fern leaves, especially when she touched them after a rain when the lingering raindrops gave a cool sensation to her hands. It was curiously invigorating and persuaded Maria to keep the planters on the windowsill, ignoring any danger of their accidently falling to the street below. Her grandmother had often warned her about the heavy plants sitting so precariously on the windowsill, for a strong wind could topple them and inflict severe injury to passersby in the street.

Small raindrops gliding on swift spring-wind currents begin to form abstract patterns on the almost deserted courtyard of the Piazza San Giovanni located directly beneath Maria's window, as people huddled together taking shelter under the awnings of various cafes around the Piazza. When sitting at her window, like sitting at an apex of a triangle, she had a view of both the Duomo and the tower on her right; slightly to her left, that of the Baptistery located at the base of the imaginary triangle. Her ancestral house was located at the corner where Via Calzaioli merged into the Piazza San Giovanni, the Piazza for which she had a slight preference due to its smaller size, compared to the vast Piazza Duomo that always seemed overcrowded with tourists.

The octagonal shape of the Baptistery, harmonious and solemn, its exterior adorned with white and green marble, was enriched with three sets of splendid bronze doors, and living in its shadow, Maria always found solace in her Christian faith. This Romanesque building of the eleventh century that Dante called 'the beautiful St. John' was a constant reminder to Maria of the importance of religious values.

After World War II, many residential and commercial buildings emerged surrounding the Piazza San Giovanni like tall, ominous looking soldiers keeping an eye on their captive. Maria's ancestral house somehow remained unscathed and managed to preserve its historic image from the post-war onslaught of modernization. While most surrounding buildings were converted into lucrative apartments and then sold individually, Maria and her family, although struggling with its upkeep, owned the entire three-story house.

Maria stared blankly at the falling raindrops that continued to paint patterns in the Piazza below as if writing an encrypted message for its observers. She sipped her hot coffee and felt the warm fluid going down her throat, unsuccessful in soothing her soul. Her mind was cluttered with wandering thoughts that appeared haltingly before dissipating, just like the disappearing raindrops below.

While her soul remained devout to her Christian faith, faith that for centuries instills in human hearts on one hand the joy of commitment to the Christ and on the other hand the fear of lack of redemption if one is not in compliance with His teachings, it was her heart that felt the stirrings of this new age of freedom. Her sister, six years younger than her, was emblematic of this growing freedom and Maria admired and often felt envious of her. She could never feel the happiness of this radical freedom like her sister did, that seemed to originate from breaking the rules of a strict religious family. Maria watched her beloved city of Florence fall prey to those who unquestioningly believed in preserving history, tradition and its values at all costs.

2

She touched the wet rim of the blue planter with her long, slender fingers and savored its grainy, rough touch on her soft fingertips. She then ran the same fingertips on the side of the window frame. The old wood frame felt reassuring, solid under her touch as if reflective of its resolute nature that had successfully overcome the ravages of time. She turned her gaze away from the window to focus on the inside of her room. It was a large room, almost thirty-by-forty feet, with a high ceiling, occupying the whole top floor save an adjoining bathroom. All corners where two walls met were smoothly rounded up and an ornate crown molding created a flawless flow between the walls and ceiling, revealing in its simplistic elegance the artistic edge of its architecture from the bygone golden era.

The Venetian shutters on two large windows facing the Piazza Giovanni, painted a soothing blue color, remained always open in Maria's room for her soul craved fresh air and she hated confined spaces. The room walls were originally painted in sunset-orange yellow that as years passed had faded to a hue that resembled the color of a golden dusk. The reason Maria's parents and her mother's parents before them left the walls untouched in Maria's room was the amazing fresco on its ceiling.

Although very old, the fresco still exhibited in its vivid colors a masterful copy of the painting of 'The Birth of Venus' by Sandro Botticelli, the original of which is held in the Uffizi Gallery. The painting depicts the goddess Venus, having emerged from the sea as a fully grown woman, arriving at the seashore. Despite its nudity, Maria's grandmother always viewed this fresco from a religious standpoint, as the nakedness of Venus suggested that of Eve's before the 'fall.'

Once landed, grandma believed, the goddess of love would don the earthly garb of mortal sin, an act that would lead to the New Eve—the Madonna whose purity is represented by the nude Venus. Once draped in earthly garments, she becomes a personification of the Christian Church, which offers a spiritual transport back to the pure love of eternal salvation. The scallop shell upon which the Venus or Eve or Madonna or the emblematic Church stood was seen by Grandmother in its traditionally symbolic pilgrimage context and to her, the broad expanse of sea was a reminder of the Virgin Mary's title stella maris, alluding both to the Madonna's name, Maria, and to the heavenly body Venus, or stella. The sea brings forth Venus just as the Virgin gives birth to the ultimate symbol of love, Christ.

Grandma often reminded Maria, the first grandchild, that she was the most beautiful baby at birth, and at her grandmother's insistence she was named Maria after Madonna. Over a very short period of time everyone called her Mary except Grandma, who insisted on calling her Maria.

To Maria, however, the nude fresco of the goddess Venus was simply a depiction of the pure love of paradise—long, flowing blonde hair, an ivory-smooth, pale-skinned and voluptuous body. Her long neck and curviness emphasized her femininity. Blown by the scented breath of ecstasy, she is carried on the soft foam by the waves of the resounding sea and she arrives, gold-wreathed, holding her long tresses in her delicate left hand, clothed in heavenly raiment.

In the daylight, the bright colors highlighting her golden hair, the luxurious garden, the gorgeous draperies of the nymph, and the roses floating around the gorgeous nude all suggest that the fresco is meant to bring pleasure to the occupant of the room. In this room, often lying undressed under the fresco, Maria saw it as a mirror and felt blessed by the Virgin.

She shifted her gaze away from the fresco and peered at the bottom of her empty coffee mug, wondering if she would celebrate her twenty-ninth birthday as a nonevent quietly, like the few birthdays before, by having a bottle of wine and dinner with her sister in one of her favorite restaurants. In her heart of hearts she wanted it to be different, something special, as it was heralding the end of her twenties. She shuddered at the thought of turning thirty the next year. A melancholy feeling arose and collapsed somewhere in the depths of her heart as she remembered how her parents used to throw a big birthday party for her when she was little; she missed her dad.

3

The sun hidden behind the rainclouds was slowly moving to kiss the horizon and she was alone and at odds thinking about her life.

She looked out and watched inattentively the columns of rain riding on the wings of swirling wind dancing around the cobblestone courtyard of the piazza beneath the house. Darkness gradually descended on the city of Florence and the streetlights began to come alive to dispel some of the increasing darkness as they flickered through the shimmering rain. The shiny cobblestones intermittently reflected the yellow light of the street lamps. A somber calm filled the empty piazza but it failed to comfort Maria's troubled mind.

Like today, every evening Maria would sit in her favorite dormer window and look out at the world below in the fading hues of the twilight. She needed this special time of day everyday to reflect on and understand a strange yearning that one day someone would bring hope to her world of disquiet but then, in the fading light, such a feeling would somehow succumb to the darkness of inevitability. Nevertheless, she needed this special hour of the day to collect her thoughts, to sort out who she was now and who she could become one day, for she always let her hope take flight to a life of laughter and happiness.

This bridging hour between failing light and gaining darkness seemed to hold hints of a premonition of her future the same way as it seemed to bring flashes of past memories. It was only when on a stormy evening a sharp, jagged lightning would strike followed by loud thunder that open, unhealed wounds would bleed old sorrows. But this was always brief as the persistent rain that would soon follow with thunder eased her mood. Maria loved the rain.

Maria and her six-years-younger sister Kathleen had jointly inherited the house from their parents. The magnificent family home, built in the sixteenth century, was shrouded in mystery. At the tall arched entrance of the house an inscription marked in a triangular-shaped stone read 1560, above the entrance gate. Rumor told that Giorgio Vasari, the author of the *Lives of the Artists* as well as the court painter and architect who built the world-famous Uffizi art gallery, had lived in this house for some time. No one knew or really cared who had started this rumor and how it came about. Since Vasari constructed the Uffizi art gallery from 1559 to 1574, and he needed a house to live in, some had plausibly believed that the great architect may have had a hand in the design and construction of his own home.

The house architecture displayed the harmonious fabric of the seductive, Romanesque, Gothic and Renaissance town that for centuries and even today continues to attract lovers of beauty. Florence continues to remain a favorite with the tourists who frequent Italy to seek the beauty of its architecture, richness of its history, but above all, its romance. Although Maria's house was not on the visitor's itinerary, its alleged historical significance had special meaning and a place in the hearts of the Zuccato sisters as well as local historians and businessmen. A wealthy businessman with alleged connections to the mafia had on more than one occasion made attractive offers to buy the house, but Maria and her parents before her could not conceive of parting with this piece of their own souls: The house had always been their sanctuary.

The chiseled and weathered sandstone of a warm amber tone adorned the front façade of the house and gave the house its lion-tawny tinge. Although not huge, the house was spacious and its four bedrooms were spread out on four levels. While Maria, since she was a baby, had the use of the top floor, her sister and grandmother shared the third floor. On the third floor, which had two separate and smaller bedrooms, both had windows but they were not the large dormer type, nonetheless offering a pretty view of the city. The second floor was the kitchen area with a dining room for the family. For formal gatherings the family used the ground floor. On the ground floor the front door entrance opened into a small lobby that joined a large sitting area adorned by heavy rosewood furniture.

The music of the falling rain brought Maria's mind to yesterday's event when she with her sister went to the railway station located a short walk away from her house in the Piazza Delia Stazione.

4

Regardless of the fact that Kathleen had to come here to find customers, she loved the Florence railway station for its history. Besides, it was a crisp spring morning, perfect for a walk and then a hot espresso in some quaint little café by the roadside. Walking side-by-side, they chatted, or Kathleen chatted, in an animated fashion and Maria with a smile listened, as she often did.

Kitty, as Maria liked to call her, was lively, she was willing to prattle all day long and she laughed easily at everything. Her sister's contemplative mood and silence disconcerted Kitty. Maria had a way that exasperated Kitty of returning no answer to her frivolous chatter. It was true that it needed no answer, but an answer all the same was what she wanted to keep the conversation going. After all, isn't that what friends do when they meet, for Kitty considered her sister to be her friend as well? Sometimes Kitty would have liked to shake Maria to bring her into the living world.

Finally they arrived at the station and found two seats in a café next to the church located opposite the station, and they ordered two espressos. "Where are you?" Kitty asked in an exasperated tone as she peered into Maria's eyes and almost whispered, "Honestly Mary, you ought to laugh more. Don't you want to have some fun in life?" She put it as a truth more than a question, but there had been plenty of truths between them that each had contradicted. Maria, however, let this one pass, only answering a question with a question: "What makes you think I don't have fun?"

Kitty in her uncharacteristic silent response simply pursed her lips and raised her eyebrows and looked toward the station building. Firenze Santa Maria Novella has one of the most architecturally significant recent buildings of any Italian railway station. Built in 1984, Florence's earliest railway station was the 'Leopolda,' designed by Robert Stephenson, the son of the man who invented railways. As Italy's first railway station, it was located outside the city walls. Four years later a second station, the "Maria Antonia," was built inside the city walls, an important innovation for the railway conceptualization prevailing in those days. Later the 'Maria Antonia' station was demolished to make way for the present station facing the church of Santa Maria Novella: a masterpiece of rationalist architecture, one of the finest expressions of the modern movement in Italian architecture.

An interesting concept, one that Kitty never failed to explain to her customers, was that once an agreement had been reached between the City Council and the state railways that Florence's main railway station should continue to be located inside the city walls, in 1932 a national competition was launched for the design of the new, what they then called, 'Travelers Building.' The Tuscan Group of architects headed by Giovanni Michelucci and included Baroni, Berardi, Gamberini, Guarnieri and Lusanna won it.

The station was opened in 1935, featuring a spacious entrance hall with its glass and steel roof structure and the main gallery, whose functional layout heralded the one later built in Roma. Its outer facings and finishing reflected the materials and colors of the city around it, while important artworks including sculptures by Italo Griselli and paintings by Ottone Rosai and Mario Romoli adorn its interior.

"You know," Maria began, putting her cup down on the table, "I've this feeling, don't ask me why, but feel strongly that today is your day and you are going to land a good client. A real prince, you know what I mean?"

"Really!" Kitty's eyes sparkled. "You think so? I do, too. Yes, I feel lucky today."

"Well, you are so knowledgeable about the history of our city, you're charming, you are beautiful and you have been working so hard," she paused for a moment as if adding weight to what she was saying and then continued, "well, sooner or later all your hard work is bound to pay off, so why not today, it's a beautiful morning."

"Oh, you're such a perfect sister." Kitty leaned forward and held Maria's hands in hers, squeezing them warmly. "We ought to go somewhere on holiday this summer, just you and I, wouldn't that be nice?"

Maria laughed and, releasing her hands from Kitty's, she picked her cup up again but before putting it to her lips said, "Let us not get ahead of ourselves. We have plenty of bills to pay and besides, we're happy here."

"Always the sensible one," Kitty pouted in mock disappointment, "live a little, have some fun."

"Tell you what," said Maria, "I'm going to let you contemplate all the fun while you are working and I am now going for a long walk. I'll see you later, at home. Don't be too late. And don't forget to look out for the prince. He is coming today, I feel it."

Maria grabbed her little handbag and slipped the black sunglasses back on, then with a little wave and a broad smile, she said goodbye to Kitty. Kitty waved back and tried to catch passing waiter's eye to get her bill. After settling the bill she got up, crossed the road and walked into the Railway Station with high hopes of finding a high-paying tourist.

5

Located in Piazza Delia Stazione, it was an impressive building that had refused to give into the contemporary and utilitarian modern architecture. Kitty always thought that the Station had soul, a vibrant energy that it emanated by bringing the world cultures to the fair city of Florence. Kitty would watch for hours the faces of different nationalities as they poured out of the station and wonder what kind of lives these people had back home. Were they blessed like she was with a centuries-old, rich culture? She would have liked to have enough money to visit some of those faraway, exotic lands she had come to know about by talking to her tourist clients. She always enjoyed those clients who would freely give information on their country and its culture.

But it had been over two weeks and she hadn't had a recent client. She desperately needed one for she hated idle time on her hands. She loved her job and enjoyed meeting strangers. But she was not overly concerned. The season hadn't yet started, for the height of summer, when tourist season moves into full swing, was still at least a few weeks away. There was something else. With the advent of low-cost informative guidebooks, tourists were not keen on hiring guides to show them around the city of Florence. People either liked the low-cost option or simply preferred their privacy or maybe both. But they missed out on so much without the help of a local guide and Florence has so much to offer, Kitty often thought. Once you take the time and spend good money to come this far, then why not hire a local guide who can give vivid explanations of art and history better than any guidebook ever could?

But today she felt confident of finding a high-paying customer. In that crowd, she felt, was the perfect customer waiting to appear any moment now. Right from the moment she woke up she felt that something extraordinary was going to happen to her that day—she was feeling lucky. Kitty walked up to a newsstand in a corner and picked up a copy of The Florentine, a bi-weekly free newspaper in English, and began to turn its pages while keeping one eye on the crowd that constantly poured out of the station. She watched attentively as the crowd came out of the station. Most were the backpacker type and she knew they could not afford a guide. Somehow she knew that she would find the right customer when she saw one.

Kitty was well aware of the fact that her outspoken approach had often lost her business. She had decided that today she was going to be a little cautious in approaching a potential client. Kitty was a free-spirited, outdoorsy person who loved the challenge of making it on her own. And that was to be a guide to show off her beloved city of Florence to those who loved art. Kitty had the lightheartedness that dependable, romantic Maria lacked.

As the crowd started to thin out, her hopes began to dwindle, but then suddenly she spotted what she had been looking for. A tall man leaning against a wall was glancing around as if he had lost something while bending over to tie one of his shoelaces. His soft brown hair draped across his forehead and his flushed face gave him a hint of casual grace that somehow appealed to Kitty. *He is perfect*, she thought, and made a beeline for him.

6

David, with an air of stylish elegance, sauntered out of the station as if he had plenty of time on his hands. He had purposely chosen a train to arrive in Florence, even though he had first flown from London to Rome to get what he had thought was a better perspective of the local flavor. And he was not that far off the mark. The scene may have not been entirely Italian in ambiance but it definitely was European. 'Excusez-moi,' 'perdoname, por favor,' and 'scusa' were some of the words uttered as people brushed past him in the emerging crowd from the Station.

He wore an off-white linen shirt with sleeves rolled up, cotton khaki pants showing signs of wear, and ankle-high hiking boots. He had thrown a light-brown sweater over his shoulders with its arms tied around his neck to keep the morning spring chill off. Slung over his left shoulder was a green daypack with a half-filled clear plastic water bottle strapped to its side and he was dragging a medium-size suitcase. He stood at six feet two inches tall and his body was built like that of a middleweight boxer and, like them, he was known for his speed and strength amongst his colleagues.

But his facial looks betrayed his general physique. His soft brown eyes always held a sparkle in them that often gave strangers the impression that he was a friendly, welcoming and considerate man, and that he was. He wore a gentle smile and offered a helping hand to whoever was in need. Despite his tough and solidly built exterior, David had a kind heart. With his tanned, slim but muscular body, angular features and head full of long brown hair, he was a glimpse of god.

He stopped and leaned against a wall to tie a loose shoelace that seemed to have come undone. A short distance away he caught sight of a beautiful woman and in her hurried gait she appeared to be on a mission. She was carrying her slender but curvaceous body on high heels with confidence like fashion models do on a catwalk. He soon realized that she was heading straight for him as she had her gaze fixed on him. Giving a final tug to finish tying up the shoelace, he pushed himself off the wall and slowly continued his walk towards the exit.

"Buongiorno e benvenuti a Firenze," her voice was placid as a summer lake. She stood blocking his way, but she wore a welcoming smile.

His response, when it came, was polite but distinct. "Good morning and thank you," David answered softly, narrowing his brow, hinting at his confusion.

"Oh, of course," she put up the palm of her right hand, covering her mouth as if suppressing a smile and then with a welcoming vivacity in her eyes, added hurriedly, "you're British. I should've realized. Let's get away from this crowd. Over here, I'm having an espresso, would you like to join me?"

David tilted his head to the side at the inappropriateness of the sudden invitation but then noticing the casualness with which she had asked, half accepted her offer and followed her to the table.

"Cappuccino please, thank you," he said, taking a seat opposite her and then with questioning eyes asked in a polite voice, "do we know each other?"

She laughed and her pearly white teeth complemented her sparkling eyes. Her tight pale-blue, low-neck sweater, matching the color of her eyes, unsuccessfully tried to contain the beauty of her youth, and faded, turmeric-colored flared trousers somehow accentuated her exuberant personality.

"*Santo Gesu*," she cried, "what must you think of me? Let me introduce myself. My name is Kathleen Zuccato and I'm a tour guide. You don't look like a normal tourist to me, you're, how shall I put it, a historian or a journalist or something like that looking to explore Florence. Am I right? Would you be interested in seeing Florence the way it should be seen and appreciated?" She stopped suddenly as if out of breath.

It was now his turn to smile. He extended his hand, saying, "David Hawthorne. And you must have read my mind because I sure could use some help in this town."

She took his broad and strong hand in hers and felt a shiver of excitement go down her spine. "Really?" She was a little flummoxed with such an expedient acceptance. "I mean," she added, swiftly realizing the ineptness of her response, "how delightful. How long you're here for? Have you already booked a hotel?"

"Wait, wait," he ran fingers through his long, soft brown hair that casually draped over one side of his forehead. "I'm not exactly a tourist. I'm here to write a book. If you want then you could help me learn about the people and places of Florence but with an emphasis on people. I would like the soul of this city through its people to come alive in my novel. Could you do that?"

"Of course I could do that. The places and people of Florence are my specialty. What kind of book are you writing?" She leaned forward, taking interest in this unusual customer. She felt excited at the prospect of this being a possible long and beneficial contract.

They waited as the waiter placed two cappuccinos in front of them. David then smiled shyly like a child would if he were caught in the middle of a mischievous act and said, "I haven't yet decided. Well, to tell the truth, I've never written a book before. I'm hoping that it will give me an escape from my incurably prosaic past illusionary life. I am hoping, you know, that Florence will be a source of inspiration to my hope to become a writer and ideas will emerge as I learn about the people and the places. Maybe you could help me crystallize my thoughts as we move forward? I know it is rather an awkward thing to ask but here we are."

She looked searchingly into his soft brown eyes that revealed a mixed message of friendliness and sadness. But it was the kindness in them that compelled her to get to know this stranger. In their depths she could sense the will of a strong heart and the frailty of a troubled soul; that intrigued her. She sipped her coffee and after she placed the cup back on the saucer asked, "I would be happy to help you but tell me this first, why Florence?"

He raised his eyebrows in a contemplative moment and, pursing his lips, responded, "Not sure, to be honest. I tried Rome first but though it has amazing history, I found that its people have restless souls. I didn't think they could inspire stories in me. Perhaps I sense an indefinable condescension in them to the stories I want to write, but Rome did not welcome me like Florence has. I know I've just arrived but I already feel at home with these warm and welcoming people, like you, for instance. I know I am making it more and more awkward for you, but I do feel that though this city is vibrant with tourists of many nationalities, the soul of this city is calm, or at least that is my first impression, even though like I said before, I have just arrived."

"Okay," she replied, stretching out the word to gain a better perspective of the situation and then uttered, "why don't we discuss my fees and I could also tell you about rates of some of the reasonably priced, nearby hotels? I take it you will need accommodations for a few weeks, maybe a few months? Oh, by the way, my long term rates are not that expensive and this coffee is on me."

They spent about an hour over coffee discussing places to visit and things to do and agreed on a flat monthly fee and then Kitty walked David to a quaint three-star hotel and negotiated a reduced rate for a long-term stay.

Walking back home, Kitty smiled at her intuitive feeling of finding luck that morning and decided to celebrate with Maria over a glass of wine at a café near her house. She wanted to share her good news.

7

The next morning the lightened eastern sky waited for sun to breach the horizon. Gradually a silvery edge of the sun appeared and it seemed to linger for a moment or two. Then the earth, shimmering in the morning's pink hues, seduced the sun and it gradually and resolutely continued to climb and engulf the blue planet in its bright sunlight.

David, awakened by the bright light streaming into his room, continued to lie in bed watching through the window the unblemished blue sky. The sunrays dancing on the red-clay tiled roofs gave a soothing warmth to his heart. It was a beautiful spring morning.

His thoughts turned to Kitty and he was pleased to have met her. His first impression was that she was charming and assertive but not pushy. He could do with some company, he thought, but he was equally pleased that they had agreed to meet again in a couple of days after he had time to settle in. An unbidden smile flickered on his lips as he remembered his discussion with her on selection of the hotel.

"Let us see now," she had said in an excited voice with her chin resting on her interlaced hands, "you're the kind of guy who needs a beautiful place and not some bland corporate hotel, am I right?

"Of course I'm right," she continued her train of thought, "but it has to be cost-effective as you may stay here for a little longer than our usual visitors."

And she was so right when she walked him to the three-star Hotel Orto De Medici, located in the San Lorenzo neighborhood of Florence, close to the Convent of Santa Apollonia, statue of David, and Cathedral of Santa Maria dei Fiori, not too far from the Academy Gallery and Chiesa di San Lorenzo. And maybe the best feature of its location as he discovered in the morning was its proximity to the Piazza della Santissima Annunziata.

David listened as the life in the street below his hotel window was stirring with morning activities and the espresso machines in scattered cafes busily poured out steamy black nectar. The rising coffee aroma wafted in through the window and David stretched luxuriously, contentedly climbing out of bed.

About an hour later he was downstairs and approached the concierge for information about the surrounding area and where he could go to have breakfast.

"The Piazza della Santissima Annunziata," the concierge at the hotel explained, "is one of the most beautiful piazzas in Florence. Arcades border the pedestrianized square on three sides. The central arcade forms the portico of the Santissima Annunziata church, which gave the square its name and at the center of the square stands a large bronze equestrian statue of Ferdinando I de Medici, created by Giambologna, a Flemish sculptor who moved to Italy in the sixteenth century."

Tall, slim, and in his late sixties, the concierge in his customary colorful costume looked more like a member of a brass music band than member of the hotel staff. He held the broad lapels of his tunic and leaned forward as if to ensure that David was listening and continued enthusiastically,

"The north side of the square is framed by the Santissima Annunziata church, a parish church founded in the thirteenth century by the Servite order. Inside are nine chapels that you must see."

"And how about some authentic breakfast in a roadside café, which one would you recommend?" asked David, a little overwhelmed by the information overload.

"Oh, for that just step outside the hotel and you will see one of the most charming cafés immediately opposite the hotel. Ask for Lorenzo and tell him you're staying at the hotel. He will take good care of you."

David thanked him and stepped outside into the soft sunlight of early morning, crossing the road to go over to the café. As he stood at the doorway a smartly dressed waiter greeted him with a broad smile. "Welcome to Florence," smiling, he offered David his hand, "my name is Lorenzo."

"David," he shook his hand warmly, "David Hawthorne. I'm staying at the hotel opposite your café."

David liked the friendly approach of Lorenzo and noticed that he was a little overweight and maybe in his forties, his pitch black hair sleek and combed back to highlight the rather large forehead that gave him an air of importance. On his crisp white uniform he wore a long apron from his waist to ankles, tied with strings around his waist, in which he had tucked away a small order book. His sharp facial features and piercing dark eyes declared his Roman heritage loud and clear. He came across as intelligent and proud and seemed witty and cordial to the brink of exuberance.

It was early morning and the café was not too busy. David asked for a cappuccino and a croissant. In a few minutes Lorenzo turned up with a steaming hot cappuccino and a pair of hot croissants on a white plate with a glass of water. As he placed David's order on the table in front of him he asked, "Did you meet my cousin in the hotel and did he tell you about our famous church over there?"

"He sure did," David answered, "and he also said I must see all nine chapels inside."

Lorenzo gave a muffled laugh as he nodded his agreement. He leaned forward by putting one of his hands on David's table and said in an amiable tone, "Look, my cousin is good but he talks a little too much. Yes, you can see all nine chapels, but the one you don't want to miss is the middle chapel, designed by Giambologna for his own tomb. The church has amazing frescoes, but most people come to see a painting that was started by a monk in the mid-thirteenth century and supposedly finished by an angel, the cause of a still ongoing veneration of the painting. The artwork depicts the Annunciation, what we call in Italian Annunziata, hence the name of the church."

Lorenzo offered another fable, "Here on the east side of the Piazza, we have the arcaded portico of the Spedale degli Innocenti, Europe's oldest orphanage. The orphanage opened in the fifteenth century and allowed women who had birthed unwanted children to leave them here anonymously by placing them on a circular stone. After they rang a bell, the stone was rotated full circle, taking the baby inside the orphanage. Fantastic, isn't it?"

Both the knowledge of the waiter and the beauty of the Piazza and its fascinating history charmed David and he felt happy to be in Florence. He'd begun to realize that he made a wise choice in coming here to find material and inspiration for his book. When David fell silent, lost in thought,

Lorenzo said, "Enjoy your coffee. If you need something, just shout for me."

David appreciated the respite and sitting in the mellow sunshine, enjoyed his buttery croissant and hot cappuccino. This was much better than greasy eggs, bacon and burnt toast, he mused. He scanned the little piazza, his attention for the moment directed more to the people wandering through the piazza than its surrounding buildings. Unlike back in his own country, here he observed that the Italians had a refined taste in clothes.

While men dressed in fitted jackets, pressed slacks and leather shoes walked with a confident gait, it was the women emblematic of trendy fashion who caught his eye. Slim and tanned bodies with sharp features clad in fashionable dresses and high-heel shoes showed meticulous attention to grooming. He appreciated nature through human beauty and artistically pleasing places and this was what he had been longing for.

He placed on the coffee table the novel, *The Painted Veil,* by Somerset Maugham he'd started reading in bed last night before going to sleep. He could not remember the last time he read a novel at breakfast. Leaning back in his chair, he closed his eyes momentarily. The soft sunrays on his face accentuated the glow of happiness in his soul and his mind created an imprint of the surrounding morning scene as a sweet memory.

A few moments later he opened his eyes to let them continue to feast on the surrounding beauty. He picked up his novel in one hand and in the other his coffee and as he allowed himself to be transported by Maugham and slowly sipped his coffee, he felt swept off on the sea of dreams. This was a magical moment, one he had been hoping to have for a long time. He preferred his mornings in beautiful and calming surroundings, alone with a good book.

Although he had left only two weeks ago, England to him now seemed a distant memory. He welcomed this feeling as he wanted to forget his past, strewn with blunders. He wanted to find moments like the present to mend his soul.

He put his book down and ordered another cappuccino. Unlike Rome, Florence was the seductress that won David's heart and soul.

8

As the day grew older, after a long and luxurious break-fast David aimlessly wandered through the various streets and piazzas soaking in their charming ambiance. There was a sense of elation in his soul and he often stopped to sit on the steps of various churches and make notes in his diary. Discovering every new piazza, he felt new windows opening up in his heart.

Realizing that it was lunchtime and he had walked for miles, feeling a little hungry he wandered back to the same café where he had breakfast and the waiter, recognizing him, offered a welcoming smile and a table in a corner.

"Buon pomeriggio, Lorenzo," David greeted the friendly waiter, trying to impress him with his limited knowledge of the Italian language from the little travel book containing useful phrases every person visiting Italy should know.

"Ciao, David," responded the waiter, "ready to experience some Florentine cuisine?"

"Excellent," David replied, making himself comfortable in his chair, "educate me, but please, I'm not in for anything heavy."

"Sure, David," he responded as he launched into his well-rehearsed speech, "you've come to the right place to taste some fantastic food. At the heart of Florentine cuisine lie four fundamental ingredients: bread that is plain, unsalted, well-baked with a crispy crust and light and airy inside, extra-virgin olive oil, without any doubt the best even for frying, grilled meat, Florentine steaks of beef, roasted or wine-braised game such as boar, deer and rabbit and lastly, of course, the wine itself. Life is sweet when you have vino. So let me start you with a glass of chilled Chianti; you know what they say, 'life is vino, my chum.' "

David chortled, explaining, "Cabaret. Life is a cabaret, my chum."

"*Si, si*, whatever," he mumbled as he flicked his hand towel over his shoulder in a gesture of mock indignation and turned on his heels, within a few minutes returning with a carafe of Chianti that he poured into a glass on the table. "*Salute*, you enjoy and I will bring a plate of something nice for you. I promise that today it will be light. Now you taste this vino and tell me if it is not life itself. Cabaret, huh?"

David smiled and picked up the wine glass, swirled it around, took a sniff of its aroma and found it to be delightful, crisp, fruity and chilled, just the way he liked it. He let out a sigh of contentment and took another sip then closed his eyes to savor the moment. When Lorenzo brought over the carafe rather than just a glass of wine, David had thought it unnecessary, but the way he felt after taking a couple of sips, he was glad he had the whole carafe to himself.

He opened his eyes and two tables away his eye caught a glimpse of something that made his heart miss a beat. A lady, sitting cross-legged in a sunset-colored dress and white shoes, one of which was dangling, hooked on one of her toes, sat reading a newspaper. He could not see her face for every time her hand appeared to pick up her glass of wine, she kept the paper before her with her other hand. What made David's heart race with excitement was the sight of the shapely, slender and beautiful hands that brought perfection to an already picture-perfect spring afternoon. He never knew that hands could be so lovely.

To him there was no grace rated as high as shapely hands. As he watched and continued to sip his delicious wine, a feeling of romance as fresh as the spring morning settled on his heart and he allowed himself to be intoxicated by this euphoria.

David wondered if she knew she was being watched. It was rather rude of him but he daren't take his gaze from her, even for a moment, for he did not want to miss the chance to see her face. Just one look was all he wanted. A lady with such exquisite hands must possess an incredible beauty. Suddenly a thought occurred to him that maybe she was aware of his rude stare and that was why she hid her face behind the newspaper. He felt a little embarrassed but it was as if he was controlled by an unaccountable and uncontainable desire to remain transfixed on those hands.

"*Crostini di fegato,*" announced the booming voice of Lorenzo and it broke David's reverie. He smiled the guilty smile of a child caught doing something impish and raised his eyebrows at Lorenzo as if impressed by the dish placed in front of him.

"Wow," he said loudly, louder than necessary, as he looked at the artistic presentation of this simple dish.

"Chicken liver on bread, my friend," explained Lorenzo, "lightly toasted slices of bread spread with chicken liver paste, capers, anchovy, chopped sage leaves, butter and a touch of saffron. Better than fish and chips, I guarantee it. Try it with your vino." And then, with his head thrown back as if in triumph, he once again turned on his heels and disappeared.

David looked at those beautiful hands again and, with her face still hidden behind the newspaper, she continued to drink her wine. His loud appreciation of lunch had not stirred her. He wondered, if he shouted Lorenzo's name, would she then look up? As he enjoyed eating the chicken liver pâté on the delicious bread and sipped on his wine, he kept his eyes fixed on those hands. Suddenly Lorenzo walked up to the lady and placed another glass of wine in front of her, removing the empty one, but even that did not reveal her face.

This was now becoming a little obsession and David found it to be an amusing game. David continued to wonder if she too was playing a game and knew that he was watching her, or rather her hands. He cautiously scanned the crowd around him to see if anyone had noticed him staring at the pretty lady but everyone was engaged in their own animated discussion. David noticed that on her left wrist she wore a shiny, dainty little watch made of mother of pearl with a silver bracelet. A silver ring set with a solo large amethyst adorned her Apollo finger. His fascination taking full possession of him, David took out his little notebook diary and started to sketch her hands.

Then to his sorrow he saw Lorenzo bringing her bill, but then the thought occurred to him that he would now be able to see her face. As she started to fold her paper and began to stand up, she somehow turned around and by the time her paper was away from her face, she had her back to David. Her slender shoulders and half-bare arms with pale skin glowing in the afternoon sun, and golden-brown, long hair down her back gave her an angelic image that would have been worthy of Omar Khayyam's Rubaiyat.

And then she was gone and David let out a sigh, a sigh of romance, the feeling of love at first sight.

9

A few months before David arrived in Florence, upon his return from the Falklands, he was floundering helplessly in the heavy seas of friends' elaborate ironies, veiled sarcasm, tiptoed malevolence, all having a laugh at one's expense, at David's expense. He did not much care what the world thought, but the negative environment in which he found himself stifled his spirit. His hands were tainted with his own blood. David doubted if life could hold a subtler anguish.

He needed an escape, a place like Florence where he had a chance to reflect and evaluate his past.

One thing was apparent to him; he could not return to his old profession, the one he had just quit, even though that is what he was best trained for and for what he was most admired. To him it was a long cold agony of traditional values. He was made to fulfill promises he never made, to live a life that was not his own. And then on one fateful encounter in the Falklands, it all came to a crashing halt. Those memories haunted David and flitted in his mind as sharp, short flashes of tragedy, never staying long enough to paint the full horrors of its intense gravity but causing sudden blindness of the soul, like a precipitous jagged lightning would to a stranded traveler sheltering under a tree while gazing at the angry sky.

In his little and lonely world, his mother was by far the most sensitive, and she knew how to transform his traumatic life to reveal his enthusiasm, his roving curiosity and discover the glow of success reflected through his latent abilities. She being of Jewish origin understood the agony of persecution as her forefathers did in the forties. She understood her son's pain and advised him to seek solace in international travel.

David remembered that his mother had also introduced him to writings of the old masters and he started to read voraciously every night—Dickens, Tolstoy, Henry James, Lawrence, Yeats, Graham Green, Edith Wharton, Dostoevsky, Keats, and Somerset Maugham—a heterogeneous mixture, for he suddenly discovered that he had read nothing for years. His appetite for literature was equal to that of arid land that is suddenly sanctified with a monsoon torrent.

David admittedly had never known anyone like her, and could hardly imagine anyone more unlike him; yet after his return a deep-down understanding was established between them. A lady of few words, she professed that he was not alone and had advocated that he with open mind travel the world to learn different histories and cultures, and latent within them their people's agonies and jubilations; to let the world and its possibilities come to him. She understood his abilities far better than he did.

Whenever she spoke, every question she asked was like a signal pointing to possible solutions, and her silence imparted a deeper understanding of her logic. Her rarest quality was a quiet radiance, which sent its beam through the dark fog of weakness and pain, encouraging one to embrace her advice and seek solace in its wisdom. Her philosophy was based on a singular assumption that the only constant in life is change and one must learn to embrace it whole-heartedly. Resistance was and always has been futile.

David remembered the way she would sit with him at the breakfast table with a cup of coffee in her hand and look at him as if trying to impart her secrets. "Life is the saddest experience there is, next to death, yet there are always new countries to explore, new books to read and, I hope, one day for you to even write one of your own," she'd told him. Seeing David take comfort in her words, she had continued, "Hundreds of little beautiful things surround us and we ought to learn to rejoice in them, then we will be able to create our own magic to bring delight and not despair. The world in front of us is a daily miracle for those who have eyes, and you are young. Get out of here, away from the daily misery, see the world and create new memories."

The advice had freed David once and for all from the incubus of an artificially pre-designed plan of regret and repentance, and sent him rushing ahead to travel Europe with a mission of no fixed objective, letting each incident of each new country create the next, keeping in sight only the lone traveler's essential sign-post, the embrace of the inner significance of the "adventure." The hidden romance of bullfights in Madrid, golden colors of magic sunsets in Provence, the exuberance of youth in Heidelberg, history and its lessons of Rome all created a thin veneer of balm on his troubled soul, but it was not until reaching Florence that his heart sensed a deep soothing calm, filled with possibilities. But this, like all the rest, merely enriched the complex music of his strange inner world, that is, until this afternoon when he saw those divine hands.

So, today was the first day that David truly felt alive and young again and though mostly inactive, the day to him was so exhilarating that he was not compelled to listen to his inner voices. Yet he was aware that when they made themselves heard again they would become impossible for him to ignore.

He had never imagined that something as simple as a pair of hands would take his breath away. And now the incredible had happened. At the sight of those stunning hands he had found a glimmer of hope in Florence; he felt free and his soul was happy. Surprised by the incredulity of the speed with which he'd found 'change,' he felt intoxicated by his own sweet and innocent happiness.

I suppose there is one friend in the life of each of us who seems not a separate person, but an extension, an interpretation of one's self, with a 'perfect chemistry,' the very essence of one's soul. Such a friend he believed he had found irrespective of the fact that he never saw her face and did not know her name. She was a vision, whose beauty could only be seen through his heart. Incredible as it was, he was in love.

He could not explain in any logical fashion to his mind as to exactly what happens at that rare find when the heart acts blindly, like the mystic's union with the Unknowable, and then something beautiful, magical, and unexplainable seems to take place. It is not a process one must explain, defend or even try to understand. It is exactly what one surrenders to, embraces and accepts, no matter what the consequences.

While in the deep recesses of his mind, the dark memories of his past dwelt like a gloomy northerly sky, and at times he was compelled to peer into the darkness; today it was the sight of those beautiful hands that were like the noonday glow of his own Mediterranean. Intangible a feeling as it may be, he was willing to bet everything on it.

How much he would have to bet he had no idea, for the twist of fate had a surprise in store for him.

10

The following morning David returned to his favorite café for breakfast, then for lunch and in the evening for dinner but there was no sign of the lady with those magnificent hands. After dinner and rather late in the evening just before closing, he could not wait any longer and summoned the waiter. "Lorenzo," he said almost in a whisper, "excuse me, but do you remember the lady, you know, the one sitting over there yesterday, you served her white wine?" Seeing his eyes widen in bewilderment, he volunteered further information, "She was wearing a peach-orange dress and white shoes and yes, reading a newspaper. She sat just two tables away from me?"

Lorenzo's somewhat perplexed gaze showed a playful disapproval, "Signore, you don't waste time, do you? She was beautiful with those amazing, large blue eyes. Have you ever seen such large, ocean-blue eyes? Only God could create something as beautiful as those eyes, as we say in Italian, *dio si è fatto quegli occhi.*" He paused for a moment as if collecting his thoughts and then added, "I think she has many admirers. Actually, I know she has many admirers. Well, I don't blame you for asking about her, we do have many beautiful women in Florence, don't we?"

So, she has blue eyes, he silently told himself. *How wonderful.* "Yes, you do have incredibly beautiful women," he said excitedly as his anticipation started to get hold of his heart and with a slight tremble in his voice he again almost whispered, as if asking Lorenzo to disclose a secret, "So you know her then? What is her name? Does she come here often? What can you tell me about her?"

"*Si*," Lorenzo's voice was resolute, "of course I know her. Lorenzo knows many such ladies but I don't ask for their names. It's not polite, Signore, and besides, it is none of my business. I keep my nose clean. And I don't mind giving you a bit of advice, you being such a good customer already, you stay away from these beautiful ladies, in the end they are nothing but trouble. They will break your heart. And you don't know Italian men, they jealously protect their women."

Someone a few tables away snapped his fingers, demanding immediate service, and Lorenzo, under his breath uttering some appropriate insults, headed in that direction.

David finished the last few drops of wine in his glass and walked back to his hotel, smiling at the concierge as he strolled through the lobby. He was hoping it was already the next day, the day he had arranged to meet with Kitty. He showered and then slipped into bed. He tried to read *The Painted Veil*, but could not concentrate so he put the book down on the side table and turned the bedside lamp off, only to toss and turn in his bed. An image floating in his head of two delicate hands called him to follow them. He could not believe that he had been in Florence only a weekend and it had already given him a reason to live. Finally and mercifully, sleep came and with it, amorous dreams of a beautiful lady with large blue eyes.

The next morning, the sunrise sky sprinkling wisps of fading pink filled David's heart with promise. After a long, hot shower he picked out an open-collar light blue shirt and khaki cotton trousers. He slipped his arms through his favorite barley-colored cotton jacket and looked at his image in the full-length mirror. Satisfied that he was not overdressed for a casual day outing and yet appropriately attired to greet his pretty guide, he stepped out of his room, hanging the sign 'Clean My Room' on the doorknob as he shut the door behind him.

At the café Lorenzo, with his hands full of dirty plates, pointed by jutting his chin towards the corner for David to take his usual table where he had placed a small 'Reserved' sign. David mouthed 'thank you' and made his way towards the table. He did not have to wait for long before Lorenzo appeared with a smile and his cappuccino.

Placing the cappuccino on the table, Lorenzo smiled broadly, saying, *"Ciao, David,* how about some egg Florentine? It is a very nice dish for the breakfast."

"Ciao, Lorenzo," David reciprocated with a smile, "sounds great but I'll have it later. I'm waiting for a lady to join me for breakfast."

"Tu non perdere tempo il mio amico," Lorenzo praised David's progress and added, "good luck."

David sipped on his steamy cappuccino and looked around the café that was already quite busy with both locals and tourists. His eyes were longing for one more sight of those delicate and deific hands but alas, no such luck. He gently shook his head as if to console his heart.

Several minutes went by and as he savored the last of his coffee he noticed Kitty entering the café and waving to him. He stood up to greet her. Kitty, after shaking hands with David, sat opposite him and smiled at the approaching Lorenzo and said to him, *"Buongiorno, Lorenzo. Un caffe per favore."*

"*Si, signora,*" was his cheery response and he raised his eyebrows at David as if inquiring if he needed another cappuccino. David shook his head and Lorenzo swiftly returned to the kitchen.

"Ah, Lorenzo, isn't he an excellent fellow?" asked Kitty.

"Lorenzo? Sure, he is an excellent fellow," David answered as he reflected on yesterday's conversation with him.

"You don't sound convinced, what's the matter?" she asked him with inquiring eyes.

"Oh, no, no. I didn't mean it that way. Of course, he is great. It is just that when I asked him something, he had to go through three successive mental processes before he could understand what I was saying. First he had to register that he was being spoken to, then assimilate the meaning and if there was any hidden meaning, and lastly to think out what practical consequences might be expected to follow if he answered. He ought be a philosopher, not a waiter."

"You are amazing," Kitty laughed and her white teeth shined like a strand of pearls. She nodded and added, "That is Lorenzo, all right."

Her short auburn hair with chestnut-colored streaks in it was spiked up and as she took her sunglasses off and put them on the table, he noticed her pale-blue eyes. Her face was small, and with her little nose with its point slightly turned up and thin painted lips in subtle pink, she resembled a doll. In tight blue jeans and low-cut white, satin blouse with a short brown jacket, she dressed like a model in a fashion magazine.

Lorenzo turned up with an espresso for Kitty and he winked at David as he put another cappuccino in front of him and in a low voice said, "*Sulla casa per voi per mante-*

nere la compagnia della signora." David understood from the wink and smile that he had brought him another coffee to keep the lady company so he simply responded, *"Grazie."* David's vocabulary of Italian words was rapidly expanding, thanks to Lorenzo.

David raised his cappuccino cup to Kitty and his heart was filled with an elation that promised a great day. "I'm so happy you're here," David said as he looked in her pretty face and added, "I can't believe that I've got the prettiest girl in Florence to be my guide."

"Flatterer," she responded and hastily added, "but don't stop."

They both laughed in unison and after a few comments by David on how wonderful her choice of hotel was they ordered breakfast. Over the eggs Florentine Kitty gave a brief account of the history of Florence to set the scene for their walking tour and after David paid the bill, they headed out of the café to start their city tour.

Their first stop was Uffizi Gallery.

11

Stepping into the expansive Uffizi gallery, David in his heart felt flummoxed but not irksome, a notion that he could not straight away understand. As he progressed through the gallery listening to Kitty, David remembered the time when he and his mom, a great lover of art, first visited the National Gallery in the Trafalgar Square in London. Standing with his mother in front of the fifteenth century painting that was considered among Pesellino's greatest, showing David's triumphal procession from Gath to Jerusalem where David holds the head of Goliath, the giant whom he has just slain, she had said, "I named you David, for I knew you would have to fight many Goliaths to survive in this cruel world."

David wondered if his mom's admiration of Florentine painters and his unwittingly finding peace in Florence had some celestial connection. Maybe that was the notion that stirred mixed feelings of inexplicable glee and a slight melancholy in his heart.

Kitty and David wandered from room to room and while to many visitors they were just artworks, to David each and every picture was like a diary of the painters' tumultuous life. They had written it in all its glory, in brilliant color.

And then he came to a painting that made him stop, mesmerized by its beauty, 'The Birth of Venus.' Kitty saw him looking intently at the painting so she offered a little background. "This was painted by the end of the fifteenth century by Botticelli, one of his masterpieces. Here you see the Zephyrus, god of the west wind, is blowing Venus to shore. There to meet her is a goddess of the seasons, waiting to clothe her. And if you look at it closely you will find that the composition is a pyramid shape, with the base reaching outside the picture. This is a trick to make the painting appear larger than in fact it is. Do you like it?"

David didn't answer for he did not hear her question. There was something in that painting, he squinted his eyes as if trying to decipher an encrypted message that stirred something deep inside his soul. *It is right there in front of me*, he mused, *but what? What is it that I am looking for*, he wondered. Then suddenly he noticed. It was so clear and in plain sight, those long, slender fingers of her right hand covering her breasts and the long golden-brown hair gently flowing over her slim shoulders in an onshore breeze. "I have seen those before," he said in hardly an inaudible voice. "Now I'm becoming obsessed," he said, this time a little louder, and shook his head as if dismissing the incredulity of his thought.

Startled by his muttering, Kitty asked, "Are you okay, David? Shall we take a break?" Kitty, having broken his reverie, stated, "We have been wandering for a few hours now and you seem to be miles away."

"Oh no," David answered haltingly, feeling as one does when accidently stumbling over a stone, "no, no, I'm listening. You're doing a great job. Yes, yes, I love this painting. It is just that this place is similar to and at the same time quite different from the National Gallery of London."

"You do talk in riddles." Kitty smiled with her eyes and with mock bewilderment added, "Whatever do you mean by being the same and different?"

"Well, you know," David hesitated as if trying to see through his cloudy thoughts, "just like here, the National Gallery in London too has a couple of thousand paintings, from Leonardo da Vinci to Vincent van Gogh. But when you go through it, you feel like a tourist, while here I feel as if someone has turned the clock back and I'm dwelling in the old Florence of the fifteenth century. I've never been drawn to a painting like this before. It is like it is speaking to me. Weird, isn't it?"

"Not at all," Kitty now smiled broadly and explained, "this place, Florence, Italy, and its people welcome its visitors with their soul and we take great pleasure in sharing the glory of our past, not just for the commerce. I have no doubt you will sooner or later find out that the people here will tell you they are passionate people. Passion is our life and it shows in everything we do and everywhere we go."

The remainder of the Uffizi tour became more animated than before as Kitty detailed not only painting techniques of the various renaissance masters but also stories of their colorful and passionate lives. After several hours that felt like minutes to David, they decided to take a lunch break. Kitty made the choice and took David to a small restaurant known for its traditional Tuscan recipes.

"Don't tell me," David put both his hands up and added, "the first course is Chianti."

A peal of laughter greeted his statement and she returned, "You catch on fast, don't you? I think we're going to get on famously."

David let his silence indicate the acceptance of the compliment. Kitty leaned forward and said, "We should do what you call 'Cheese and Wine' to keep our lunch small, for we have more places to visit."

"Ah," David raised his hands again, "cheese and wine would be great, but I ought to warn you that I am a Scotsman from the MacDonald Clan and very proud of it."

"Okay," she laughed again, "excuse me, Mr. Scotsman of the MacDonald Clan, we will do cheese and wine but Tuscan-style. So we will order a special assortment of Tuscan cheeses and wines in three steps. First, we will have a glass of white wine Vernaccia di San Gimignano accompanied by Brie and Acacia's honey, then a glass of red wine Chianti colli Saenesi with Pecorino do Fossa cheese and strawberry in aromatic vinegar, and last but not least, a glass of red wine Brunello di Montalcino Tiezzi with the local Pecorino cheese and figs and so you don't go hungry, also some antipasti, we call it Affettati Mist."

"So much for the small lunch," David responded, laughing, "I should have known that there is no such thing as fast food here, it is all slow food and honestly, I love it. Let's call it a day and enjoy the afternoon with a lesson in Tuscan cuisine. Let's add food and wine to people and places. I'm all for it."

The afternoon lingered on and David let the intoxication mixed with the romantic surroundings bring him to a relaxed mood as he enjoyed Kitty's laughter and occasional touch on his forearm. He felt it was the start of something good, something special.

12

The remainder of the week was just as exciting as the first visit to the Uffizi gallery. By the time the end of the first week arrived the bond of a pleasant friendship grew stronger between Kitty and David, as evident now by the playful banter in their discussions and especially at the lunchtimes that always involved a bottle of Chianti. Time flew as David found Kitty's company both comforting and pleasant and he wondered if he could find a way to make a living from his writings, as then perhaps he could have means to settle down in Florence. But so far, although he had learned a lot about Florence, he'd had no luck in putting a book together.

His inspiration seemed to have vanished with the absence of the vision he once had. He wished that he could have just one more chance to see those gorgeous hands and this time he wouldn't be so shy and ask for her name. Lorenzo could not help him with a name and she never turned up again at the café.

"Listen, David," Kitty said wiping the corners of her mouth with the white cotton napkin and paralleling her knife and fork on her plate, "I've known you now for several weeks and if you find life dull on your own during the long summer days of weekends, then give me a call. I don't mind coming out for an hour or two, you know, just for the company. We won't call it business so there will be no charge. Okay?"

"That's very kind of you," said David, also putting his knife and fork in order, "but it won't be necessary. I think I already have tons of material to start thinking of a plot for my book. It's time I made a start. It would be good to be on my own to get my notes sorted out. Who knows, I might surprise you one day and hopefully soon with a chapter or two."

"Good luck then," she concluded with a smile and pushed her chair back to leave. "Sorry, I won't stay for the coffee if you don't mind. I've a few things to do this afternoon before the weekend so let us meet again on Monday, say at nine in the morning."

David stood as she did and kissed her on both cheeks as customary in Italy. After she left he enjoyed his coffee and reflected on the past few weeks. He thought of writing a historical novel for after all, Florence was full of colorful history. But then decided against it because he knew he was not a historian and would not be able to do justice to the subject. Maybe a fiction novel then, he wondered. But about what, he scratched his head. He studied the bottom of his coffee cup but there were no answers for him there. Then suddenly a thought came into his head that started to take root. A blend of a fictional and historical story based on Florence and its famous families, maybe the Medici family. He liked the idea but could not build further on it. After paying the bill he decided to walk the six blocks to his hotel to let the fresh air generate some new ideas.

When he arrived at the hotel he felt tired but relaxed. He went up to his room and fell into his bed without taking off his clothes and boots. He stared at the ceiling and then closely inspected his new and upgraded room that the hotel management gave him a week ago at no additional charge, being a long-term guest.

A long low-ceiling room, with white-paneled walls hung with watercolors of varying merit, curtains and furniture of faded slippery chintz, a French window opening on to the back of the hotel building and a crazy balcony, from which, on one side beneath it, one could catch a glimpse of a small and neatly laid lawn and shrubbery edged with a successful herbaceous border. On the other was a not-too-successful rose garden, with a statue of a cupid with bow and arrow poised on the edge of an incongruously "arty" small blue-tiled pool.

By the French window was his favorite seat, a chintz armchair, a small side table piled with a few novels and picture-magazines, and the armchair could recline so he often lay outstretched, his legs crossed, his hands and mind occupied with a novel.

The room itself was not too large but not too small either. An open-plan small sitting area with a small desk and a sofa and couple of chairs were adequate for a single person to read or watch television. He liked the en suite bathroom that had a reasonable size glass-enclosed shower cubicle, which he thought was rather extravagant for European standards.

What he admired most was the taste Italians had for color. Three of the inside walls were painted a dull turmeric color to give it a stately appearance that complemented the hand-carved woodwork around door and window frames that were broad, ornate and painted in pearly white. The fourth wall seemed like the feature wall with a fresco, no doubt a copy of an old Renaissance master.

After another walk later on in the day and a light dinner, he called it a night and went to bed early. He had a satisfying week and he wanted to be in the privacy of his room to reflect on it. Slowly his eyelids closed and he allowed himself to drift into a dream world of romance and contentment.

It was early in the morning and the dawn brought a new day and with it new hopes. The sun was on the point of rising, but he found the room still dark and silent. The stillness of early morning slumbered everywhere, the curtains were yet drawn over the French window, and little birds were just twittering in the tree outside his window, whose boughs drooped like green garlands over the stone wall enclosing one side of the yard. Footsteps stamped from time to time in the cobblestone street outside; all else was still. David liked unhurried mornings and enjoyed the music of silence.

He wanted to wander about on his own discovering new streets, different piazzas to continue his euphoric feeling in this newly found world. Deep within him he was quite aware that whatever he was feeling was fragile and nothing but a temporary balm to mask the pain of his deep wounds that could erupt at any time. But he was thankful for small mercies and willing to take his days one at a time. In his professional world he had learned that in the survival of the fittest, the operating word is survival. Survive he must, for he had expectations, mostly from himself.

Since his mind was not quite ready for him to be cooped up in his hotel room contemplating story plots, he decided to get out for his favorite sport—people watching. He also knew that creativity was out there in the open and not hidden in his mind, he must continue to explore and he felt confident that he would know when to start writing.

"There are a couple of great places to people-watch in Florence," Kitty had told him one day, "but for my money the best one is the Piazza della Signoria—if for no other reason than the artwork surrounding the square, which is always fabulous-looking. Enjoy your weekend time there, especially now that summer is almost here. This gorgeous open piazza is the front yard of what was once the ruling Medici family's home, the Palazzo Vecchio, which has a 'David' replica standing at its entrance. The Loggia to the right of the Palazzo Vecchio is a fantastic outdoor sculpture gallery." Kitty had warned David, "The restaurants lining the square are mostly overpriced but you should feel free to bring your gelato cone in from elsewhere to enjoy the view while you eat. If you want to splurge on a sweet treat with a view of the Piazza della Signoria, I strongly recommend getting a ciocolata calda at Rivoire and sit outside if you can find a table. Give it a try, you won't regret it."

David had no idea of the miracle that was waiting for him at the Piazza dell Signoria.

Book II
Florence, Italy

Summer 1983
"Life devoid of love is like a year without summer."

13

It was the summer solstice marking the first day of the season of summer. Summer had finally arrived and Florence was now even prettier, like a young girl who has grown into a beautiful woman. Long summer days, especially weekends, lay ahead for David to explore indulgently and lazily.

David did exactly what Kitty had once recommended and found himself an outside table at Rivoire and ordered a ciocolata calda. As the sweetness of the very first sip stimulated David's taste buds, he had to admit that the ciocolata calda of Rivoire gave a completely new meaning to hot chocolate as he knew it back in England. There was simply no comparison.

As he continued to sip his hot chocolate the scenes from the story of *The Painted Veil*, the novel he had ignored for the last couple of weeks and finally had finished last night, started to drift around in his head. He wondered, if Somerset Maugham had spent some time in Florence instead of Paris like he did, then maybe he would not have been so harsh on Kitty Fane. He felt sorry for her husband who had to suffer humiliation from her adulterous affair but eventually admired her courage when she was compelled by her awakening conscience to reassess her life and learn how to love. At the end of the book David felt that love is not a mere infatuation or sporadic feeling of lust; no, it is way beyond that, as Somerset beautifully articulated in his book. Love is something one learns from personal sacrifices, from giving unconditionally, and from having no expectations.

As David was lost in his abstract thoughts suddenly something gave a jolt to his daydreaming, bringing him back to the land of living. It was a sight of nothing less than a slice of heaven. A tall and slim body, wrapped in a body-hugging, pale blue, knee-long cotton dress, silver bracelet shimmering in the late morning sun on her wrist, golden hair caressing her slender shoulders, she with her back towards him was slowly walking with a natural swagger of hips away from his table.

It was she. It was as if the world around him had frozen and faded away in some dull tone of colors and only she existed, in her colorful attire, moving away. He could not have been mistaken for her last vision was burned in his mind. It was definitely she. Graceful, sensual, heavenly, and many other such words floated around in his mind but the one that gave him the second jolt was bill. Yes, bill, that was what he needed to settle and quickly for there was no way he was going to miss out on this rare chance provided by nothing less than heaven itself to see her face. Ciocolata calda would just have to wait. He spotted a waiter and waved at him frantically to get his attention as he tried to get up.

As he hurriedly got out of his chair, he almost tipped it backward as someone caught it and said, "What's the hurry? So you took my advice, that's great. Come on, sit down and finish your ciocolata and offer me one, too. I could never pass on such a wonderful treat." He looked at Kitty as if seeing her for the first time and tried to say something plausible to get away but could not find words and all he could do was to continue to wave, but now slowly, for the waiter as he was doing before to get his attention for the bill.

While he was still standing the waiter came over and David said meekly, "Another ciocolata calda, grazie."

By the time he sat in his chair and glanced back at the piazza she was gone, having disappeared into the crowd. His heart sank. He let out a sigh of disappointment over the missed opportunity. He said in a forced, casual tone, "I thought we were not going to see each other again until Monday?"

"You sound disappointed, "said Kitty with a frown, "aren't you happy to see me? Whatever happened to all those compliments, beautiful guide and a wonderful companion? Oh, maybe I interrupted something, did I? Look, I was concerned about you, you know, being alone on the first summer weekend. I've told everything about you to my family and we would like to invite you to a little party at our house tomorrow evening. Nothing extravagant but it would give you something to do. Besides, my family is wondering whom I have been seeing for the past few weeks."

"Well, thank you," David composed himself and, touched by her generosity, this time responded in an amicable tone, "I'm not much of a party man. I find them rather awkward, you know? But do thank your family for it."

"Oh, come on," Kitty stressed every word with insistence, "it is not really a party as you are thinking, just a few family members and some close friends. I promise we won't keep you more than an hour. Please, don't let me down? I promised my family I would bring you to this party, please? For me?"

"Okay, okay." David laughed as he saw her sitting there with puppy dog eyes batting at him. "Give me the address and I will see you there. Now enjoy your ciocolata and don't even ask me about my book for I've not yet started thinking about it. It is harder than I thought it would be."

"I can see that. It seems there is something else on your mind that is keeping you from finding ideas for your book. We've known each other for quite a few weeks now. Come on, you can share it with me. I know that expression on a man's face; it says I'm lost and I need to talk to someone. Well, lucky for you because 'someone' is here."

David saw no harm in sharing a fantasy, for that it really was. Besides, he had no clue who the lady with the beautiful hands really was, and Lorenzo was not going to help him find out. If the truth be told, he was beginning to believe that he really was destined not to meet her as he now had two missed opportunities, including the one a few minutes ago. He explained to Kitty about the amazing hands and how he came so close a few minutes back to finding her.

Kitty let out a peal of laughter and after a few moments, when she found she could speak again, she said, "I took you for some tough military guy. You know, what I want is what I get. You really are a softy, a helpless romantic. Well, tell you what, I will help you find your lady, especially when I am the reason you lost her this time. We can work together on it and who knows, you might be lucky. Another of my talents as a tourist guide."

They both laughed this time and after David, with a sweeping gesture of his hand, implied they forget about such talk, they both engaged in discussing the people they walked past, offering comments on both appearance and clothing.

14

The next morning David knew exactly what he had to do to prepare himself for the evening party. Apart from shying away from frivolous chitchat, the main reason David wanted to avoid Kitty's party was because all he had were travelling and casual clothes and none were suitable for going to somebody's house for a drink, especially when you're invited for the first time. *Europeans can be so formal*, he thought. So, in the morning, he set out to do some shopping for clothes. His height presented a problem, but in the end he managed to find some pleated beige colored slacks, a smart casual black shirt and a tailored jacket. He also bought a pair of black shoes for he thought his hiking boots would not have been appropriate.

Exactly at six in the evening he turned up at the address that Kitty had given him. He looked at the front of the house and could not believe that Kitty and her family lived there. It was magnificent, that was the only way he could describe it. The house, situated on a cobblestone street not far from the flagstone-covered beautiful Piazza San Giovanni, was enormous in size and in its appearance gave an inspiring impression of its past glory. The heavy wooden front doors with chunky brass studs stood tall and prominent as if proud of their heritage and, at the same time, seemed burdened with the generations of secrets they held. He delicately ran his fingertips on the weatherworn wood as if to become a part of its past.

The exterior was tawny and ornate, little affected by time, as if protected by some force-field. Its aging four walls refused to let its burdened back sag under the weight of its substantial roof, mighty turrets and heavy gargoyles, proudly standing erect as a sturdy soldier stands motionless guarding the palace of his master.

David glanced up and noticed a windowsill on the top story, with two large planters holding green fern swaying in the gentle breeze. The mellow evening summer sun was reflected in the light of tiny water drops clinging to the ferns, sparkling intermittently like twinkling stars on a clear night. He stepped back to get a full view of the house and was impressed with the turreted roof structure that gave the house a stately ambience as if in its architectural language it was speaking of its important past.

David walked up to the silver-grey gleaming front stone steps of the large door and pressed a bell mounted on the right side of the doorframe, obviously a modern addition that was a practical alternative to beating the door with your knuckles. After a few moments the doors opened and Kitty stood there with a bright smile.

"Welcome," she said in a somewhat formal voice. David noticed that she was dressed in a turmeric-yellow dress that accentuated her pale blue eyes. She looked stunning in her dress and David realized that he had never seen her before in anything but trousers and jackets. *She should wear dresses more often*, he mused admiringly. He handed over a bunch of flowers that he had picked up from a florist on his way and gave her two customary kisses on both cheeks. As he bent slightly forward to kiss her, he noticed the pendant around her neck. Although the necklace strand was made of simple knitted leather, what caught his eye was a magnificent pendant in the middle that looked like a large and very old coin. It was made of gold or something similar that had a shine like rich bullion.

"Amazing," David said as he stepped back after kissing her, "I've never seen anything like it."

"Wow, that is the best compliment I've had this evening. I didn't know you admired me so much. Thanks very much." She said this half appreciatively and half mischievously, for Kitty never took anything seriously.

"No, no, I was admiring your pendant," David said hurriedly and then instantly realizing his mistake, corrected himself, "and of course, you look beautiful, too. You always look beautiful."

"Liar, but you are a handsome liar," she continued with her little bonhomie and stepped aside to say, "do come in."

"I didn't know it was a dress-up day, I hope I'm not too casual," David said to continue the friendly conversation.

"Actually I should have warned you," said Kitty softly as if imparting a secret, "today we're celebrating the Ferragosto, you know, the Assumption Day, when we Italians rejoice with a little bit of a feast to commemorate the Virgin Mary being taken up to heaven. Actually, it is not until mid August but Grandma finds August too hot so we celebrate it early. We do it only because of my grandma for she is rather religious, more superstitious, if you ask me. Anyway, nothing formal; we have a few friends and family members and I'm sure you will enjoy yourself."

They walked down a paneled corridor that was both wide and airy and it led to a large drawing room with a tall ceiling. Everything in it was harmonious in color and tone, from the tall Coromandel screens, the old Chinese rugs on the floor, and the early Chinese bronzes and monochrome porcelains, to the crowning glory of the walls, hung with pictures of excellent prints of Renoir, Degas, Monet, and Anne-Louis Girodet de Roussy-Trioson—the "Bathing Women" of Renoir, the somber and powerful "Young Woman with the Glove" of Monet, and a landscape of a peculiar hazy loveliness by Alexandre-Hyacinthe Dunouy.

Opposite the entrance from the hallway into the drawing room was a solidly built spiral staircase with a silky finished oak handrail and on the landing was a large portrait of Marco Polo. It looked rather a misfit with the rest of the paintings but then so did all of the Chinese collection. Well, there might be some curious connection, David thought, and decided to ask Kitty at some other more appropriate time. There were very few people, some of them were divided into small separate groups and engaged in various animated discussions.

There were but twelve, yet, somehow, as they gathered around, they gave the impression of a much larger number. Some of them were tall, many were dressed in white, and all had a sweeping array of presence that seemed to magnify their persons as a mist magnifies the moon. David gave them a slight nod as he went past them. One or two bent their heads in return and the others only stared at him. Then David noticed a grand old lady in very expensive-looking clothes sitting alone beside the window, staring at the people in the crowd, mouthing words no one could hear. The strangest thing of all was that not a soul in the house, except David, seemed to notice her and her habits, or seemed to wish to approach her. She was there for everyone to see but somehow being ignored, no one pitied her solitude or isolation.

A joyous stir was now audible in the drawing room, gentlemen's deep tones and ladies' silvery accents blending harmoniously together. The people were speaking in Italian and David regretted coming for he realized he was going to be a misfit in this gathering. Kitty saw the disappointment on his face and a mischievous smile crept down from her eyes to her lips and she whispered, "Don't panic, you've me to talk with all evening and besides, once I introduce you to some of these people, they will be happy to practice their English on you. But first you must say hello to my grandma. She is there sitting in the big chair by the window."

Kitty held David's hand and led him across the drawing room where they stood together in front of the grandmother. David looked at her, a woman in her late seventies, perhaps early eighties who must have been extremely pretty in her younger days, sitting erect in a big wing chair with a glass of white wine in her hand. Her silver grey hair was meticulously combed and neatly tied in a bun with a dark maroon ribbon around it at the nape. She had worn a voluminous dress draped all the way down to her ankles in a spreading scarlet silk festooned with black lace, on which her long arms and frail hands rested like some regal lady sitting for a portrait. She had stature without height, grace without motion, presence without mass. Slender and simple, remaining soundless, she was somehow always in the line of the eye; the crowd always bowed when they made eye contact with her.

An expression of almost insupportable haughtiness in her bearing and countenance broadcast that she was not to be trifled with. She had Roman features and a double chin, disappearing into a throat like a marble shaft: These features appeared to David not only exaggerated and gloomy, but even furrowed with pride, and the chin was sustained by the same principle, in a position of almost preternatural erectness. She had, likewise, a fierce, hard eye. She mouthed her words in speaking, her voice deep, its inflections pompous—unendurable, in short. One had to know her and her ways to tolerate her for then, David was sure, she might even have been amusing.

With her strident dress and intonation she seemed an incongruous figure in that drawing room, where everything was in half-shades and semi-tones—but then when she began to speak he knew he had found the real mistress of the house. Her voice was clear and she spoke with seriousness in her tone. What David found inescapable were her stern mocking eyes under the stylish arch of her black brows.

"Grandma," said Kitty to her, "this is David, the one I have told you about."

David extended his hand and shook her frail but deceptively firm hand. She pointed towards a small chair next to her and with her eyes asked him to take a seat.

Before Kitty could take a seat on the other side of Grandma a young man dressed in full police uniform approached Kitty, kissed her hand and then took a quarter of a turn in a stiff police-like fashion and addressed Grandma, "*Buona sera, signora.*" Grandma simply nodded and did not make eye contact with him, presumably either because she detested authorities or didn't particularly like this young man. The young policeman, after his greetings, equally ignored Grandma and, with an air of confidence that held a hint of arrogance, waited to be introduced to David.

David saw a suppressed smile on Kitty's face as she cleared her throat a bit as if getting ready to make an official announcement and said, "David, allow me to introduce to you my friend, Ispettori Affonso Di Liberto. We went to school together; he, as you must have gathered from his appearance, is from the Polizia di Stato and his name literally means 'noble and ready.' One day he is destined to become the Commissari Capo. Am I right, Affonso?"

"*Si, Signora*," he said with a straight face, raising his chin just a little as if adding a touch of defiance to his arrogance. She then turned toward the young Ispettori and David noticed that Kitty was now having a tough time hiding her smile as she finished the introduction by saying, "And Affonso, this is Mr. David Hawthorne from England, my all-time favorite client."

"*Buona sera, signor*," Ispettori returned, clicking his heels and one more time stiffening his body as he came to attention stance. David shook his hand and said, "How do you do?"

This seemed too much for Kitty and she said to David, "You talk with grandma for a few minutes and a little later I will introduce you to some of the people here. Let me take Affonso to talk with other friends, okay?" Kitty turned on her heels and grabbed Affonso by his arm and hurriedly stepped away to mingle with the crowd. Grandma made a slight gesture with her chin as if disapproving of Kitty's friendship with the Ispettori.

For a while there was an awkward silence between him and the grandma as she glanced at him from the corner of her eye and David felt he was being examined. He noticed something in her face that puzzled him. Her eyes that were calm and peaceful when he was introduced to her a moment ago now looked disturbed and he could see a little trembling in her hands if something was bothering her. David wondered if she disapproved of his presence.

15

David, with a little formal smile on his face to avoid this awkwardness, slowly turned his glance towards the small crowd in the drawing room and in a casual fashion started to scan the people.

They dispersed about the room, reminding him, by the lightness and buoyancy of their movements, of a flock of white-plumed birds. Some of them threw themselves in half-reclining positions on the sofas and ottomans, some bent over the tables and examined the flowers and books, while the rest scattered in small groups around the large room. All spoke in a low but clear tone, which seemed habitual to them.

Affonso, like a toy soldier saying hello by clicking his heels to various people, with his stiffened body moved around the crowd like a mast on a sailboat. David noticed a short and obese man dressed in a rather formal white suit with a white tie and a sky-blue handkerchief protruding out of his top jacket pocket, holding an unlit cigarette in his right hand that he waved in the face of a tall, slim lady as he engaged in a serious monologue.

There was a pair of men that seemed out of place for they were dressed informally in a gathering that seemed to have made an effort to dress up for the occasion. They were in denim blue jeans and half sleeve shirts, boots, and without jackets. Then a tall, heavy man in an off-white linen suit holding in his two cupped hands three glasses of red wine approached them and carefully handed over two glasses while starting to sip from the third glass. David noticed that the man in the linen suit, prior to joining the other two, sent an inquisitive and yet stern glare at him as if displeased or even maybe angry at his presence. There was something about the Europeans he never could grasp completely, something about how opinionated they were and how easily and overtly they could express their feelings towards foreigners. He at times found this to be rather disconcerting and it did not appeal to his reserved nature.

The next time the man in the linen suit gave him a look of blank ferocity, David purposely smiled at him in an attempt to neutralize his inexplicable feelings towards him. He turned his face away and pretended to be busy talking with the other two while David had a feeling that the man had been keeping an eye on him. David felt more amused than frustrated by his attitude. David studied the man in the linen suit a little more closely.

He was commonplace in complexion, features, manners, and voice. He was of a large size and of a big build. His eyes, the usual blue, were remarkably cold, and he certainly could make his glance fall on one as trenchant and heavy as a cleaver. But somehow the rest of his person seemed to disclaim the intention. Otherwise there was only an indefinable, faint expression of his lips, something stealthy—a smile—not a smile—he tried to discern it, but he could not comprehend it. It was unconscious, though just after he said something, it intensified for an instant. It came at the end of his sentences like a seal applied on the words to make the meaning of the commonest phrase appear absolutely inscrutable. He looked like a successful businessman as evident from his clothes but his mannerisms declared him clumsy and boring. David could see that he was obeyed; yet he inspired neither love nor fear, nor even respect. He inspired uneasiness. That was it. Not a definite mistrust, just uneasiness, nothing more.

It was not till after a few minutes that his attention was diverted again to the man in the off-white linen suit. He then seemed to be quite irritated and pointed his finger in anger in the face of one of the two men. David liked his physiognomy even less than before; it struck him as being at the same time disconcerting and conceited. His eye wandered and had no meaning in its wandering. This gave him an odd look, such as David never remembered having seen in any man he knew before. For a well-built and not an ugly-looking man, he repelled him exceedingly; there was no power in that smooth-skinned face of a full oval shape, no firmness in that aquiline nose and small cherry mouth, there was no thought on the low, even forehead, no command in that blank, beady eye. David, for an unaccountable reason, developed a dislike for the man.

His gaze drifted now to a couple in a corner that were perhaps in their early sixties and they with their hands clasped if in supplication were intently gazing into the face of a tall priest who was talking more with his hands than his mouth. Every now and then he would spread his hands as if giving a sermon.

David realized there were no children around and the ambiance was subdued with discussions in muted tones.

Suddenly the grandma looked squarely in his face and in a tone like a fortuneteller, was foretelling the future as she said, "You should not be here. Nothing good will come of it.

I don't mean to be rude but listen to an old lady who speaks from experience and heed her warning, if you value your life then don't meddle in what is not your business. Leave while you still can. This is not your town and this is not your family. Be like other tourists, see the city, take some pictures and return to your home and family. Do you understand me?"

David was so startled by this that he could not respond and simply looked at her blankly. He could not really grasp everything she had said and struggled to understand her sudden outburst. He hadn't said anything to her to offend her so was he unknowingly staring at someone in the crowd that he shouldn't have? He thought he ought to respond and explain that he had no intention of intruding, had he known it was a private affair, and besides, her granddaughter had insisted on inviting him here. But Grandma's face once again had returned to that formidable stern expression that was not open to comment.

David decided not to respond to the old woman for he thought by saying something to her things may only get worse. It is hard to change older people's minds. He felt uncomfortable sitting next to her and wondered if he should leave and looked around for Kitty. He chastised himself for letting himself be dragged into this unsavory situation and flicked an imaginary speck from his pleated slacks.

Suddenly his eye caught a glimpse of something that took his breath away. Resting on the banister of the landing was that heavenly hand adorned with a delicate silver bracelet sparkling now and then in the interior light of the drawing room, the image of which was engraved in his soul. The hand slowly glided down the banister and the lady gradually descended down the staircase. David with bated breath saw her as an angel emerging from behind a silvery cloud.

She had worn a faded, lemon-yellow dress that created an amazing background to her golden locks and piercing blue eyes. Around her neck was a necklace with a large black Moonstone pendant resting against her ivory-white breasts. She at the bottom of the stairs casually and with an air of indifference glanced at the crowd and walked straight up to where David was sitting.

"Good evening, Grandma," she said in a honey-sweet voice that was soft and mellow.

"Meet my other granddaughter, Mary," Grandma said in a voice with a hint of exasperation as if reminding him that he ought to leave now. David stood up and shook hands with Mary and the mere touch of her hand thrilled his heart and sent a shiver of excitement down his spine. "I'm Kitty's friend, David."

She simply glanced at him momentarily and nodded as if saying that his presence there was of no consequence to her and then, taking a seat on the other side of Grandma, she spoke in a soft voice, "Do please sit down. Kitty has told me quite a few things about you and she seems happy to be working with you. She said that you're quite a catch!" She laughed so quietly that it went unnoticed by Grandma and then she added hurriedly, "I mean as a client, for it is not usual for her to get a long-term client like you. You know, in her business the daily tourist is more the norm."

David slowly sat back down and in his heart thanked his lucky stars that he was invited to this little revelry. "I'm happy to have found you," he returned, and realizing the mistake he'd just committed, he flushed and faltered, "I mean her. I'm happy to have found Kitty. She is a great guide."

Mary suppressed a smile at his flustered state and to ease him said, "Kitty tells me that you're a writer and have come here to write a book. How fascinating. What is it about?"

"Oh, she exaggerates," said David, smiling, "I'm not really a writer but hoping to become one, and I'm still not sure what the book is going to be about as I'm waiting to be inspired." David wanted to add, until this moment, but kept that pleasant thought buried in his heart.

David was so engrossed in his talk with Mary that he paid no attention to the continuing glare from Grandma, who now interjected, "You can't buy inspiration by hiring a guide. Inspiration is not out there waiting to pounce on you; it is within you, but you must search to find it."

"You're absolutely right, Grandma," said Mary, leaning towards her. "The history of this city is filled with people and their stories that are so inspirational. Don't you also feel that just by being here and taking in its ambiance one could feel inspired? And you have arrived at the right time of the year, spring."

"Right time of the year?" David asked in a voice that showed more excitement at having found this opportunity to speak with Mary than interest in what she said.

Mary suddenly looked a little contemplative and suggested, "If you want to see Florence pure as a virgin, visit us on a spring morning. If you seek new meaning in life, then come experience the energy the city exuberates in summer. If you would like to heal the wounds of your heart, return in the last days of autumn. In the spring, love blossoms under the unblemished blue sky, in the summer we forgive and rejoice in life, in the autumn, we remember those who are no more."

"And winter, you said nothing about the winter? What happens to the city in winter?" David asked.

"Huh," was the short and sharp response from Grandma. After a brief pause, as if taking time to reflect on Mary's remark, Grandma turned towards David and said, "Winter brings death to the city and to its inhabitants' souls. You don't want to be here in winter."

Mary looked at David beseechingly, and in that moment he felt the barriers of ice typical between two strangers melting. Mary then stood up and giving David a slight smile, she went over to where the three men were engaged in a spirited discussion.

He had a million questions to ask and wondered if he too should join the three men and listen in on her conversation. Kitty was beautiful, but the beauty of Mary, her sister, was so rare that it was beyond his comprehension. Kitty returned and sat next to him. David leaned towards her and in a whisper said, "Why didn't you tell me that you have a sister? I just met Mary. She is the one with those beautiful hands I told you about."

"So, stop drooling," Kitty returned with a suppressed laugh, "isn't she beautiful?"

Their conversation was curtailed as the man in the off-white linen suit approached and the next words he heard from Grandma plunged a dagger in his heart. "David," she said in a formal, almost stern tone, "meet Mary's husband, Antonio."

16

After all the guests one by one thanked Grandma for a wonderful time at her party and left the house, Kitty announced she'd like to escort a quiet David back to his hotel for she fancied a little walk after being cooped up for hours with mostly ancient people, as she referred to the old folks. Mary kissed Grandma and Antonio goodnight and went up to her bedroom.

She sat on the edge of her bed and felt a strange, inexplicable and unaccountable feeling rising in her heart. *What is happening to me*, she wondered as she rubbed her forehead with her hand. She let the scene replay in her mind of her coming down the stairs, familiar people mingling and then seeing an angel sitting next to her grandma. Who was he? Could he be the liberator of her soul? But Grandma did not approve. She normally could discern right from wrong, well, most of the time. She did not stop Antonio from getting his way, but then there is always the exception to the rule. Mary noticed Grandma was almost hostile towards David. Could she be right?

Mary stood and walked to the open window to absently stroke the fern. A cool breeze blew in and it felt soothing on her cheeks. Her hair played on her shoulders, giving a pleasant sensation to her skin. She closed her eyes and the image of David floated in. She imagined herself on a tropical white sandy beach, wearing nothing but a sarong and walking hand-in-hand with David, splashing warm blue water with her feet. The sun was setting on the horizon, spraying purple on the calm surface of the ocean. The only sound was that of waves gently lapping at the shore.

Then Mary opened her eyes and did what she had not done for a long time: put her favorite music on, the disc she had hidden away in her closet and not played for years. In her opinion, Dvorak's Cello Concerto was the most darkly romantic music you'll ever hear, tinged with a shade of melancholy and coming from the soul, very moving. She adored it. As the music started to build and filled the room, she stood in front of a huge, full-length mirror and gazed at her image. She slowly swayed with the music. Her soft silk yellow dress billowed out while she twirled and twirled like whirling dervishes and she liked the slight rush of breeze around her exposed, smooth legs. Her eyes were now half closed as if she was in a dream world and was descending into a trance.

At every turn her eyes would meet with the eyes of her reflection and she would smile, admiring those almond-shaped blue eyes. The large blue eyes had a subtle sparkle in them but mostly they showed a veiled sadness that was mysteriously appealing. To her the image in the mirror was not her but her inner self that was free, exciting, youthful and a lover of life. Gradually and involuntarily her hands caressed her body and one by one she removed all her clothing. She stopped and took stock of herself naked in the huge mirror.

She did not know what she was looking for as she moved closer to the floor lamp till its golden light covered her. And she thought, as she had thought so often, what a curvaceous, almost voluptuous body, smooth and unblemished, rather perfect thing the body of the girl in the mirror was, naked, somehow a little unsatisfied, and incomplete.

She was tall, with slender shoulders and slim arms, and she had a certain fluent, natural grace that might have given her that beauty men found irresistible. Her breasts were full and ripened and her flesh was fresh with a gleam like that of young girls. Her skin was ivory like delicate porcelain, but in summer, faintly tawny; her limbs had a certain natural elegance, her body a full, attractive richness, but it lacked something. Instead of being happy about her ripening beauty, she was sad. Sad because trapped in that youthful body was a prematurely aging, dissatisfied and disappointed soul lacking real womanhood, for she had never experienced free love.

Suddenly she hated it with a rushing fury, the wasted beauty. She looked in the mirror's reflection and she knew she could not hate her for she was victim like her. In her still lingered hope. As her eyelids became heavy the mirror gradually looked increasingly opaque and she had a hard time keeping her focus.

She caressed the image with her slender fingers. She then pressed her body against it to embrace her, to comfort her. She would fight for her freedom. She would strive for liberation. She warmly kissed the lips of the fading image, turned and walked to her bed. She felt angry and helpless for those who professed to care for her were the very same people who had plunged her into darkness. And they remained an integral part of her family. How does one fight one's own family?

She slipped into her nightdress and went to bed, where she sobbed bitterly. And in her bitterness burned a cold indignation against Antonio, and his sweet talk and his money, against all the men of his sort who deceived a woman about even her own body. Unjust. Unfair. The sense of deep physical injustice burned to her very soul. She yearned for freedom but it could be a long wait, a very long wait, she thought.

The drizzle of rain was like a veil over the world, mysterious, hushed, and not cold. She lay in bed over the covers, letting the coolness of the night soothe her body, soul and mind. She had to wait. The street below was silent, still and secret in the evening drizzle of rain, full of the mystery of closed front doors of apartment buildings, closed cafes and half unrolled awnings. In the dimness of it all cobblestones glistened naked and dark as if they had unclothed themselves, and the silence on earth seemed to hum with Dvorak's Cello Concerto. A song of waiting, waiting for the angels to descend to earth. Waiting. Waiting.

She was born to wait.

17

When Kitty turned up next Monday to reconvene their guided tour, David's mind was no longer on sightseeing. The only sight he wanted to see was that of Mary, he was besotted with her beauty. He wanted to know more about Mary but realizing its inappropriateness suppressed all his queries and he tried focusing on what Kitty was explaining. After about an hour while they were having a coffee break Kitty asked, "David, I hope you don't mind what I'm about to propose," she paused to take a sip of her coffee, keeping an eye on David's face, as he was lost in his own thoughts. She resumed, "I feel as if I've know you for years. It is like we have been friends for a long time, I feel so comfortable around you. You have this, how should I say it, very likable personality, you know?"

David smiled, blushing slightly, for he was uncomfortable about receiving compliments. Encouraged by his smile, she continued, "Don't ask me too much about it, but all I can tell you at this time is that Mary and Antonio are going through a difficult phase in their marriage and who isn't, eh?" She placed both elbows on the table and rested her chin on the balled-up fist of her right hand as if in a thinking mood. Lowering her voice, she added, "I think it would do Mary good if she got out and about a bit. What I don't know is how Antonio would feel, for I don't want Antonio to be hurt in any way. He is a great guy, you know? He is so unselfish and unconditionally supports all our family as if it were his own. I do love Antonio."

"I'm not sure what you're asking?" said David, emphasizing every word, seeking better clarification.

"You're great company, funny, sophisticated and a gentleman. I have asked Mary to join us for lunch today, I hope you don't mind?"

David was intrigued and felt a flush of mixed emotions as blood rushed to his cheeks. He wanted to respond immediately but then a sudden impulse of prudence restrained him from releasing his exuberance. He continued his silence for a few more moments. "Did you hear what I said?" Kitty peered into his eyes, for she seemingly thought he would be pleased with her suggestion.

"Mary is to join us for lunch," he said hurriedly, as if coming out of a daydream. "Yes, that would be great. It would be nice to have lunch with her. With both of you, I mean." He then leaned forward and asked in a soft voice, "What kind of marriage problems?" Suddenly realizing that was too personal a question, he quickly corrected himself, "Oh, pardon me. It is not appropriate for me to pry like this. I was just being curious, but you don't have to say anything. And please don't misunderstand what I said earlier about her hands."

"I knew it; you're a perfect gentleman. No, I don't mind telling you a little more about her marriage," Kitty said contemplatively and added, "but it is a long story and I'm not sure you would be interested."

"Look," David said in a casual tone that showed more concern than keen interest, "you said we are good friends, and that we are. So simply as a friend, if it helps to share, then I am here to listen to you."

"Okay, but don't let Mary know that we have had this discussion. Mary may not approve but I am sure it would help her if she could open up with friends."

"Let us get more coffee first," said David, attracting the attention of a passing waiter and ordering two large cappuccinos. They waited until the coffee arrived and then after the waiter left the table Kitty said, "Our lives are attached to the ancestral house you came to visit over the weekend. This house has been in our mother's family for generations and our mother just like my grandma love this house. But my father, God rest his soul, who died in a car accident, was a gambler. Actually he was in the merchant navy and spent half his life at sea, but somehow succumbed to the curse of gambling. That was his obsession and to a point that he lost not only all the family wealth but also his job. The luxury of living in this large house was cursed with its high cost of maintenance and after he lost his job, he no longer could support us and look after the house maintenance."

Kitty paused as if gathering her thoughts, and to give her a little extra time, David interjected, "I thought you were going to tell me about Mary's marriage?"

"Oh, I will," she answered, "but all this is tied so intricately with this house that you need some background on it first."

David simply nodded and Kitty resumed with, "Things got so bad that Dad started borrowing money and got himself into massive debt from which he knew there was no recovery. Mother at first did not know that Dad had been borrowing money to feed his obsession and when she later found out there were several quarrels between them. She tried to remind him of his responsibilities as a father, as a husband, and pleaded with him to quit this ugly habit and make a fresh start. And he promised to do so many times but never could quit the habit."

David could see in her face a hint of both anguish and veiled anger. He realized that talking this over with a friend could be beneficial for her so remained quiet and let her go at her own pace.

After a couple of sips of coffee she let out a sigh of relief and then said, "You're the first person I've told all this information. Are you sure you don't mind?"

"Look, if it helps you then please continue, but if it upsets you then we could do it some other time. I am pleased that you consider me a good enough friend to share information about your family."

"Well, thank you. I would rather tell you the whole thing now before Mary arrives. I remember those ugly days when Mother would go into a deep depression due to mounting financial problems and being unable to maintain the upkeep of the house and Dad would promise her that his luck was about to change. Mother was fast running out of the savings she had accumulated over the years. Then as time passed things went from bad to worse."

Kitty fell silent and David could see sadness in her moist eyes. As a sign of friendship and support, he touched her elbow and Kitty responded by placing her hand over his. She lowered her eyes in reflection and then raised them again with renewed determination and said in a steady voice, "I'm okay. Sorry. I do want you to know about us."

"Take your time," said David, slipping his hand from hers and picking up his cup of coffee.

Kitty took a deep breath and continued, "Dad had started to steal from Mother and when she found her jewelry was missing, she cried. It was then she realized that he had reached bottom. She did not know to whom she could turn so in desperation she asked her mother, my grandma, to come and help. Grandma, who lived in a small house in Sienna, sold her place and moved in with us, primarily to give moral and some financial support to Mother. Dad was very upset with his mother-in-law for moving in as she is not an easy lady to live with and he often talked about asking her to leave. He also started to insist on renting out a part of our big house to raise some income or selling it altogether. But like her ancestors, my mother's soul was in this house, so giving it up or sharing it with strangers was not an option for her. Grandma stayed and fully supported her daughter and her views."

Kitty looked past David in a contemplative mood as if reliving the past and said, "The wretched house, we were entombed in it and because of it wrapped by misery."

David allowed her a few quiet moments to compose herself by asking her to excuse him and he left the table to find a washroom.

18

David returned to his table where Kitty was sitting in an uncharacteristic somber mood. David noticed that their waiter was following him a few steps back. As he took his seat opposite Kitty, the waiter arrived. With an air of indifference, he approached the table and placed two glasses of water that he seemed to have forgotten with the coffee earlier and without saying a word, turned on his heels and disappeared back inside the restaurant. David ignored both waiter and water and gave all his attention to Kitty.

Kitty picked up the narrative, "Dad was trapped in a house surrounded by four women and he started to stay out all day and most evenings, God only knows doing what. And then the inevitable happened. The moneylender, who had so generously loaned money to Dad, demanded that his money be repaid with interest, which by now amounted to an exorbitant sum, saying he needed money for his own business. The moneylender was actually the head of a family-run business of several very successful bakeries and he, due to kindness or perhaps because of old family ties, had been loaning money to Dad but obviously there was a limit to how long he could continue to give. The only means by which Dad could pay such an amount was to sell the house and Mother obviously was not having any of it."

Kitty suddenly stopped and glanced around as if worried about airing her personal affairs in a public place, or perhaps she was not certain if she wanted to tell the remainder of her story. David waited for her to resume but a thought struck him that maybe the sudden death of Kitty's father in a car accident had left them this huge financial burden and maybe Kitty hoped to ask for financial aid from him. If she did, David thought, it would strain their relationship and besides, he wanted to keep himself free of all ties so that he could come and go as he chose. But then on the other hand, deep inside he knew that if Kitty were to ask for help, he would not be able to say no. He knew that he had not left himself with much choice and let the events unfold with time.

"What I am about to tell you," Kitty said, lowering her voice, "must remain between us. You promise?"

David suddenly realized that he was getting in too deep, and he had no idea where it may lead. "Listen, Kitty," he said, placing both his hands on the table in front of him as if to emphasize what he was about to say to her, "I'm glad that you shared some of your family history with me and I am very sorry to learn about your family's hardships. I of course will not be forthcoming with this information when we lunch with Mary, but I'd rather you didn't divulge anything you feel sensitive about or that is very personal to you."

Kitty smiled and with a sweep of her hand, as if saying she was not concerned, responded, "Of course it is very personal, and I don't go around divulging such information to everyone, but you, David, you're like family to me. And I feel safe with you in sharing my past."

David had unsuccessfully tried to stop Kitty from divulging any further her family secrets but realized she was determined to disclose it all. He nodded to offer her encouragement to continue.

"Of course the moneylender, being a good friend of our family, knew the situation and realized that Dad could never pay him back so he offered a solution." Kitty's eyes shot left and right as if distrustful of this public place and then suddenly added, "Mary's hand in marriage in exchange for writing off all the outstanding debt was the offer he made. The only problem was that the businessman who handed all this money to Dad was not someone Mary was in love with and besides, he was fourteen years older than her. Mary was seventeen and he was over thirty-one. I'm talking about Antonio; I'm sure you gathered that by now?"

David had no idea of the circumstance under which Mary and Antonio had married and he suddenly felt very uncomfortable. The dislike for Antonio that he instinctively felt at the house party now suddenly took firm place in his heart. His jaw tightened and eyes narrowed to suppress a feeling of anger that he was afraid would mix with his dislike and turn into hatred towards Antonio. He did not want such thoughts as he considered them a poison to the heart and generally did his best to avoid them.

Kitty had not yet finished and taking David's silence as an invitation to continue, she said, "Of course I was only eleven at the time and did not appreciate what was going on in our family. Dad readily accepted for he did not have a choice and somehow convinced Grandma that for the sake of keeping the house she should convince Mother, who was dead-set against the offer. Dad knew if there was one weakness in Mother and Grandmother it was the fear of losing the house so he built his argument on the basis that as much as he disliked the age gap between Mary and Antonio, he believed Antonio was a great catch as he had unconditionally offered to look after the whole family. Learning from Dad that preserving the house was a pivotal point, Antonio sweetened the deal further by offering that after his marriage to Mary, he would provide financial help for the upkeep of the house so the family could continue to live trouble-free.

"Finally Grandma capitulated and she and Dad put enough pressure on Mother to accept the offer and in her weaker moment she too gave in and Mary at the age of seventeen was married off to the successful Antonio. Mother could never forgive herself and after the marriage went into a deep depression, blaming her mother for selling Mary off to keep her house. There were several heated arguments between my mother and grandmother. But this did not last for long for Mother only a month after Mary's marriage committed suicide."

"Please, Kitty," said a now wild-eyed David, "I'd no idea. I understand your family's pain and would do anything to help. I don't know what else to say except that I feel so sorry. Please, you don't have to say anymore, and you can trust me, your secret is mine."

They both fell silent and he thought that was the best way to calm their roused emotions. After several moments passed it was Kitty who spoke first and simply said, "Thank you. Thank you for being such a good listener and such a good friend."

"You're welcome." was the obvious and customary response that David uttered as an automatic reaction without any way of knowing that this friendship was going to cost him a whole lot more than he had bargained for.

19

David looked over Kitty's shoulder and saw Mary coming towards them. Suddenly for David time stopped and everything around him moved in slow motion. Mary in a pale blue dress seemed to be gliding on air with her long hair flirting with her bare, slender shoulders. His heart began to race, he could hear his heart beat and for a moment he forgot the sad story narrated only a few minutes ago by Kitty. He let out a deep sigh of intense pleasure that only his heart could feel. But Kitty saw his face and a broad smile appeared on her lips as she turned around to wave hello to Mary.

Fortunately the café was busy and that created a light-hearted atmosphere. Throughout lunch he kept the discussion focused on Florence as a city of history and intrigue and encouraged Mary to talk about her interests. He soon realized that the two sisters were poles apart in their demeanor. Mary was the very image of sophistication with an aura of mystery around her. She was quiet and soft-spoken and very much aware of the space and people around her. Unlike her, Kitty was loud and outspoken and it was emblematic of her character to speak first and ask for forgiveness later, if necessary.

David found it rather awkward to talk with Mary in the presence of Kitty, and somehow felt that he really could get along better with Mary if she were on her own. He noticed that Mary had an eye for fashion and jewelry and was wearing that amazing necklace again. Finding this to be an opportune time to satisfy his curiosity, he asked Mary, "I hope you don't mind me asking, but I find your necklace, in particular the pendant, both charming and intriguing."

"You mean unusual," she corrected, seemingly pleased that David noticed her jewelry.

"Is it?" asked David with sincere curiosity.

"This particular one actually belongs to Kitty and I'm only borrowing it for a while, but I had an identical one that I had made into a charm bracelet for my husband and he wears it all the time. The unusual part has to do with this pendant and not the whole necklace. I'm surprised Kitty did not tell you about it. It is actually a rare gold coin found by our great-grandfather during one of his deep-sea scuba diving trips. He only found two and gave them to his wife as a memento and now for the last four generations they have been in our family. I guess you could call this a family heirloom as we treat it as one."

Kitty interjected as Mary, grasping the pendant in one hand, showed it to David, "Our mother said that these are priceless and were once appraised as very valuable items but that was several years ago."

"Wow," said David looking closely at it, "I didn't know they were this important or expensive. It would be fascinating to find out their history and what they are worth now."

"Are you interested in it?" asked Kitty excitedly. "Everyone likes them but they are not for sale, you know. Our family would never part with them."

The conversation then switched to David's plans and the sisters offered various ideas on what David could write about and as often happens, it turned out to be a pleasant lunch for everyone. As they concluded the meal, Kitty covertly mouthed thank you to David and he acknowledged by simply smiling back at her. After saying goodbye to the Zuccato sisters, David strolled back to his hotel, reflecting on the luncheon conversation.

Every time the image of those beautiful hands appeared in his mind, the way her slender fingers delicately picked up the coffee cup and the way she, holding her necklace strand, had leaned forward to show him the pendant, the color rose in his cheeks. He remembered the moment when accidently his fingers touched hers when they both at the same time had reached for the sugar ball. The tingling sensation of that touch like the wafting sweet smell of jasmine in the cool evening air was still with him.

Mary was everything Kitty said she was, a product of an unhappy marriage and dissatisfied youth. Although her beauty was distracting, it was unable to completely veil the vulnerability she showed every time she tried to make eye contact. Her beauty of skin had no doubt won her many admirers but David was certain that her soul had not yet experienced the beauty of life that is found in living without fear and free. David was convinced that Mary might have found happiness as experienced by momentary pleasures, but she had yet to find the contentment that only a free-spirited soul could know.

David could empathize with her for he himself had known the sorrows of a dysfunctional family life. He wondered if he could help Mary and in that could find solutions to his own problems. Is that what his mother was trying to say to him when she asked him to explore the outside world with an open mind, he wondered. But then he reminded himself that Mary, happy or not, was a married woman and his involvement regardless of his good intentions and his clear conscience could still be misconstrued by some as interference. Most jealous men would not understand his good intentions. And this was the old-fashioned and traditionally manacled world where a Catholic marriage and its vows were taken literally when the priest sanctified the marriage by reminding the newlyweds and those in attendance that 'what God has joined, men must not divide,' followed by the General Intercessions, and then, if the sacrament of marriage was being celebrated within Mass, the Liturgy of the Eucharist.

The whole affair, David mused, was as serious here as if one was being condemned rather than celebrating love. *Why are the religious values of some,* he wondered, *so insecure and rigid that deliberation and moderation to better fit the changing times and evolving needs cannot be easily accommodated? Every religion prophesizes happiness so why then such a rigid frame of a multitude of rules that over time has brought unhappiness?*

Religion is not something one is born with, its values are taught and that is exactly how it ought to be rather than being imposed, as generally seems to be practiced by most old-fashioned generations that allow themselves little if any freedom of thought. Why could we not follow the fundamental values of all religions, which are similar regardless of different labels, and focus on those rather than how to practice them?

Many thoughts swirled around his mind without his successfully being able to latch onto any particular one. All he knew was that he remained fascinated by Mary and though he knew it would be inappropriate to befriend a married woman, he was willing to take a chance to help Mary. His heart was making commitments his mind could not deliver.

20

Mary did not overtly show it but found David to be someone with whom she would like to spend more time. She recognized that David would not reveal his feelings and harbored deep resentments from his past, for every time the conversation drifted towards his family he wrung his hands as if trying to hide his panic and quickly changed the subject. He was not the carefree and free-spirited man roaming the world, or a Casanova out for conquests, as Kitty had her believing; he was a complex man and behind his strong exterior was a lost and innocent child screaming for help. She found him to be intriguing and would love to have another opportunity, preferably on her own without Kitty, to get to know the real David.

Kitty walking alongside Mary saw her lost in her own thoughts so shook her arm and said, "You look happy. Did you enjoy meeting with David, isn't he a nice man? We should get out more, to meet people. It would be good for you. Look, if you're worried about Antonio, I'm sure he wouldn't mind as long as we go out together, so what do you say, shall we do it again?"

Mary gave her a look as if not understanding her and said, "What is there for Antonio to mind, he is my husband, not my master. Besides, there is nothing wrong in meeting with friends."

"So, it is settled then. We will go out again; it will be so much fun. Oh, I'm so happy, Mary, that you like David.

He is more than a client to me now; he is a friend." "Yes, we can go out again," Mary repeated, "provided we tell Antonio everything, and if he wants to join us then that much the better. No secrets, understand?"

Kitty's shoulders dropped as if she were disappointed at hearing this and she responded, "I'm not trying to do anything wrong. I love Antonio. He is so kind to us. All I want is a little happiness in your life. God knows you are due for some." Kitty put her arms on Mary's shoulders and in an amicable voice said, "No matter what, I'm quite aware of the fact that Antonio is your husband and I would not do anything to hurt him or you. He is kind, generous and he is family. He will always be family."

"Glad to hear it," Mary murmured and they continued their walk back home.

That evening at the dinner table, Grandmother addressed Antonio. "Today I received a message from a dear friend of mine who lived next door to me in Sienna," she paused as if reflecting on her conversation with her neighbor and then added, "she has taken a bed fall and fractured her hip. She has a nephew who looks in on her now and then but I would like to send to her a care package. I would take a train there but I don't feel strong enough for the journey. Could you find some time to make this trip?"

"Oh, you should," Kitty chimed in, "Mary and you should drive there. It is just over an hour's drive on Autostrada. It would be fun for both of you."

Mary shot Kitty a glance of disapproval and suggested, "We all could go. Don't you have an old friend who moved from here to Sienna?"

Antonio, showing little interest in the friendly banter between the sisters, looked at his watch and then addressed their grandmother, "I'm sorry but I cannot get away due to business commitments. This week we are doing stocktaking and I'd better stay here to keep an eye on it. I could go next week if it is not too late or better yet, why don't we let Mary and Kitty go? Maybe your old neighbor would appreciate a little female company anyway, wouldn't she?" He then said to Mary in a polite tone, "Why don't you take my car and enjoy a weekend away? It would do you good."

With no objection, his suggestion carried. The next couple of days Kitty remained busy showing David various sites in and around Florence and Mary made sure that Grandmother called her neighbor to let her know that Mary and Kitty would be arriving late Saturday morning. Mary insisted Grandmother not ask her neighbor to put them up for the weekend as she knew the elderly woman was not too mobile and besides, Kitty and Mary would be better off in a small hotel nearby.

Everything was planned for the Saturday trip, or so she thought.

21

It was Friday morning and as the sun breached the horizon, David was filled with renewed hope. Since the lunch with Mary and Kitty, he'd had a hard time casting the image of Mary from his mind. An imprint of her was carved in his soul that, with guilt, could fade, but enhanced by surging passion, could never be erased completely. At times it bothered him that he was preoccupied with this fantasy of befriending a married woman but nonetheless, the feeling gave him a strange kind of thrill.

With the bright sunrise, once again his heart was filled with the juvenile hope of meeting Mary again. It is an interesting notion that at sunrise the world expects new promises from a newly appearing sun. David was up at dawn to have a brisk morning walk and to enjoy afterwards a hearty breakfast. Kitty had told him that she was going away and needed Friday to clear up other commitments prior to the weekend. He had Friday to spend alone. After a long walk and feeling hungry, he found his favorite corner table and asked Lorenzo for something substantial for breakfast.

"You're indeed very strange," said Lorenzo, standing erect like a school teacher and continued, "if it is eggs, bacon, sausages, and hash browns you are looking for then you are not only in the wrong café, you are in the wrong city and indeed in the wrong country. Breakfast in Italy is very light, you know, just a cappuccino or coffee with a pastry, and we say cappuccino e brioche or a piece of bread and fruit jam.

It is not customary, Signor David, in Italy to eat eggs and bacon or that sort of heavy food at breakfast. In fact, no salty foods are consumed at breakfast, generally speaking. But to make things a little different, I will bring for you cornetto: a croissant, a very light pastry filled with delicious jam and cream."

David smiled and responded, "Okay Lorenzo, whatever you say, but make it a few cornetto, maybe a small basketful, not just one, and a large coffee, I'm really quite hungry this morning."

Lorenzo now looked briefly around and leaned closed to David's face to say in a whisper, "If it is something special you are looking for this morning then I think I have just the right thing for you. Your special lady, you know, the one you asked about a few weeks back, is sitting only four tables away behind you. You went right past her when you came in." He then picked an imaginary speck of dust from the table and flicked it away then left David to consider his next move.

David did not turn around to look at Mary for he thought that such a move could be construed rude, so he sat for a few moments contemplating how to approach Mary's table. Then he decided that when all else fails, honesty is the best policy, so he stood up, turned around and went straight to Mary's table and said, "I'm so sorry; I did not see you when I came in. I don't mean to intrude but since we are both at the same place, and if you are not waiting for someone to join you, then may I buy you breakfast?"

"Wow, what a big speech for a little breakfast." She then gave a small smile that David found very attractive as it made two well-placed dimples in her cheeks. "Yes, I would be delighted to have breakfast with you. Do sit down." Mary pointed to a chair opposite her. David pulled out the chair and sat himself down and no sooner had he made himself comfortable than Lorenzo was upon him. "Here is your cappuccino, Signor, and a basketful of cornetto to follow. The usual for you, Signora?"

After receiving a nod from her, Lorenzo turned on his heels and left as they both smiled. David did not enjoy small talk but felt that he had to start the conversation, so said, "I see that you're wearing Kitty's necklace again or is it yours this time?"

"You really are obsessed with this necklace, aren't you?" Mary smiled as she gently touched the pendant and added, "Actually mine is not with me anymore as I gave it to Antonio."

David noticed a flicker of sadness in her eyes as she mentioned Antonio's name. The cup of coffee she had just lifted hardly touched her lips before she put it down again.

"A pendant to Antonio? What on earth would a man do with a necklace?" David asked with exaggerated surprise.

"Look, David," she paused for a moment, "this may sound odd but we don't really know each other well. You and Kitty are good friends and she is a great girl and my sister, so we should keep this breakfast short."

"I'm sorry, I didn't mean to pry," David quickly responded and added, "I was just being polite and it was Kitty who thought you needed a friend. I'm sure if she were here she would be delighted to see us together. My intentions are honorable and I'm simply trying to get to know you a little better but if that bothers you—" he started to get up and did not finish his sentence as Mary interjected, "How old are you? Sit down and please don't make a scene. You look so young, and you seem so little acquainted with how women feel being talked about in public. Look, no matter what Kitty might have told you, I'm fine. She wants me to turn into a teenager again, but I'm a married woman. Please, I don't mean to offend you but it would be best if you took a little less interest in me. It is an old saying that 'all is not gold that glitters,' and in this case I do fear there will be something found to be different to what either you or I expect."

22

David kept his gaze on his cup of coffee and he involuntarily smiled as Mary talked. In his job he had been thrown many a times into life and death situations, but he could not recall anything this tough. He considered what Mary had just said. Finally he said, "No need to worry about me, I'm old enough to survive on my own. And I'm just being friendly because you are the sister of my friend. I also believe that both of us are adults and free to choose our acquaintances. But hey, if you feel troubled by my presence then I will leave you alone. Just say the word and I will disappear."

She met David's gaze and replied, "Okay, you can stay. I was just trying to be careful, for your sake. Italian men can be very jealous, and you don't know Antonio's temper. Anyway, like you said, you're Kitty's friend, and there is no harm in all of us getting together, is there? I shall be away for the weekend anyway and upon my return maybe we could arrange another lunch."

As she mentioned the weekend he gave her a faint smile so she asked, "What's so funny?"

"Oh, nothing; go on. You were talking about us having lunch again."

"It is just that I feel awkward coming between you two," she hesitated for a moment and then added, "I do not know exactly why but I feel vulnerable when it comes to relationships. Besides, you would laugh if I were to tell you my superstitions about such silly things, not that I am very superstitious."

"That sounds interesting. What kind of superstitions?"

"This is silly and sad but when I was a little girl," said Mary and suddenly her expression changed to reflect an introspective mood, "only four years old or so, I one night heard my mother say to my father that she had heard about him flirting with some other woman while she had been busy nursing and raising his child, and if this rumor were to be true then she would kill herself and her child too, leaving him to live with their blood on his conscience for the rest of his life. Those words left me feeling that it was my fault for straining their relationship and though her voice might have disappeared from my memory, to this day I remain sensitive to people's relationships and I guess as a result, I'm not a person who likes to socialize."

"Well, if it puts your mind to rest," said David carefully so as not to appear too forward, "I am no more than a client to Kitty. Sure, she is friendly and we have a few laughs together, but there is nothing between us. To be honest, she is not my type and besides, I am not looking for a relationship, so relax about Kitty."

She seemed to read the glance, answering as if its import had been spoken as well as imagined. "Yes, yes, you are right," said she, "I do take things too seriously at times. I know it, and I don't wish to imply anything by what I said earlier, I assure you. I'm just nervous, and that is the truth."

"There is nothing to be nervous about," he assured her, "we haven't done anything wrong. Not yet anyway. No, no, I'm just kidding." David saw her relaxing and in the hopes that this meeting may yield a meaningful friendship, he added a serious note to his jocundity, "Let me avow this to you. Sometime back, someone very special once told me that in the course of one's life one will often find himself elected the involuntary confidant of his acquaintances' secrets. People will instinctively find out, as I have done, that it is not your forte to speak of yourself, but to listen while others talk. I feel that you listen with an innate sympathy, comforting and encouraging because it is unobtrusive in its manifestation. What I'm trying to say is that from the day I met you, I have believed that you are a good listener and, for what it's worth, so am I."

"Who was this special person, your mother?"

David's mouth opened in surprise, "What? How did you…?"

"Never heard of women's intuition?" she laughed and then hurriedly added, "Okay, don't get serious on me. I did enjoy your company the other day and would be happy to have breakfast with you. But I'm not going to share anything about myself till I get to know you a little better. Tell me about yourself. Tell me about your job. No, tell me about your family. You have a ring on your finger, so I take it you are married. Where is your wife? Tell me about your parents and the place you were born."

David twirled the ring on his finger contemplatively and pursed his lips then responded, "Actually I'm not married, never have been. This is just for protection. You know, when one goes to bars and such places. I don't want to waste time with people I don't know."

"Very interesting," Mary murmured with a grin, "so tell me about your family."

"This is what, the third time we have met?" David asked, "Yet I feel I can tell you anything about myself. You are different. I mean that in a good sense. You're open and honest."

"Well, thank you. But you're avoiding my questions."

"You've heard, haven't you, that time is a gift to be spent slowly, only the evils of temptation hurry it through. If you consider giving me your time then I may be tempted to bare my soul to you."

David recognized that Mary was interested in learning about his past and his family but he didn't want to open old wounds so, changing the subject, he tried to humor her. But she mistook it for flirtation and a look of seriousness reappeared on her face as she scolded, "Don't wish for what is not attainable. To wish is to hope and to hope is to expect. And I do not want you to have any expectations from our friendship for I'm a married woman."

And thus, difficult as it may seem on the surface, a friendship developed between the two, the consequences of which were yet to be discovered by the passage of time, far beyond their comprehension. It seems that fate is never kind to those who surrender their all to love.

23

Early Saturday Grandma had prepared a big food hamper that included her homemade antipasto, pasta sauce, assortment of local cheeses, some fruit and a few packets of pasta.

The summer morning was sunny with a little cool air. The vivid blue sky was like a clean slate, without a cloud in sight. Mary did not get much chance to drive around in Antonio's old Alfa Romeo Montreal in Florence, but whenever she did drive the Tuscan countryside, either on her own or with Kitty, she savored it. Mary loved driving and she loved the old Alfa Romeo. Antonio would never let anyone but Mary drive his favorite car.

Loaded with the food hamper, picnic basket and small overnight suitcases, they set off after an early breakfast. As Mary maneuvered the car through the narrow streets of Florence and out towards the country, Kitty turned to Mary and suggested, "Let's not take Autostrada, it's always busy. Let's instead take the country roads, we aren't in a hurry anyway."

"You read my mind," said Mary as she accelerated towards the city limits.

"I've a confession to make," said Kitty, with her trademark mischievous grin, "I've invited David along. We're picking him up at the next crossroads."

Mary suddenly braked hard and the car came to a screeching halt along the roadside. She turned to Kitty, looked her square in the face and demanded, "What? Are you out of your mind? Antonio would have a heart attack if he found out. No, no, you must apologize to David and explain that he cannot come with us."

"Oh, please," she pleaded, "it's part of my business. I promised to show him Sienna and what better opportunity than this? Look," Kitty said in an appealing tone, "we won't bother you at all. You do what you have to do with grandma's neighbor and I will take David out for sightseeing. We won't get in your way, oh, please?"

"And who is going to explain this to Antonio?" asked Mary, shaking her head. "He wouldn't like it."

"Well, I won't tell him if you won't. It will be our little secret. David is with me and we will be spending most of the time together so you need not worry about being seen with him. I assure you, we won't interfere with your visit to grandma's neighbor. Okay? Please, Mary?"

Mary rubbed her forehead and took a deep breath. A few minutes later the three of them were on their way to Sienna.

24

It was a lovely summer day and the rolling Tuscan hills under a brilliant, unblemished blue sky made both Mary and David let out in unison a sigh of contentment. Following this they both laughed and David said, "I hope you don't mind me coming along. This is so beautiful, and so different from the English countryside."

"Different," Kitty asked, "in what way?"

"The sky here is so vast that it makes the vista expansive, magnificent."

"I'm glad you joined us," said Mary, as she slowed the car for them to enjoy the countryside, adding, "but I'm afraid I will not be able to spend much time with you two. But do enjoy Sienna, it is a beautiful city."

Making many stops at various scenic places, they finally arrived in Sienna in the early afternoon. Mary pulled over by a roadside to let David and Kitty out and leaning out the window, said to Kitty, "Hey listen, let's get together for dinner. Where shall we meet?"

"Oh, I know," said Kitty with her usual exuberance, "we'll meet at Ristorante La Pizzeria di nonno Mede. Remember the place, we were there last time we visited Sienna." She then turned to David and said, "This is a charming pizzeria that has outdoor seating in front of one of Sienna's best views—the Duomo, a historical center in the hills of Sienna. And the menu, oh, the menu includes an extensive variety of Pizze, Ciaccini, that is Mary's favorite, Focaccine Ripiene and of course Calzoni."

David indicated his agreement by simply smiling while Mary shouted back as she drove away, "Okay, we'll meet at seven, see you then." David and Kitty waved adieu to Mary and then disappeared in a crowd heading for Piazza del Campo as Mary went off to Grandma's neighbor's house.

"The first thing that we should see," explained Kitty as they walked together, "is of course Piazza del Campo, the tourist place par excellence, then the Palazzo Pubblico and the Torre del Mangia, the Baptistry, and then we shall call it a day or it would be too tiring. But, as we tour these sights, pay attention to the color of the various frontages and the roofing, as it makes the city landscape coherent, congruous and rather unique. Sienna has not changed in appearance from the Middle Ages, and walking through its streets is to travel back in time, in the search for a golden age. Trust me when I tell you that Sienna is the only Italian city left that preserves this sublime past."

It took them several hours to see these places and David decided to climb atop the eighty-eight meter-high tower of Torre del Mangia to witness the spectacle of the vast view of the entire city, while Kitty, who happened to meet an old friend, or maybe an old flame, stayed back to entertain him over a cup of espresso.

Later as the sun moved towards the west, the shadows lengthened in the Palazzo Pubblico where David and Kitty sat at an outside café enjoying a glass of wine and crowd-watching. Many cafes and souvenirs shops surrounded the place without damaging its beauty. The slight slope of the silhouette of the tower del Mangia in the Palazzo Pubblico, surrounded by impressive houses, made the scene picture-perfect and David was in its awe. Scanning the area, David said to Kitty, "Let's check out some of these shops, just to get an idea of what people are buying."

After settling the bill for the wine, they took a stroll, and David commented, "Hey, this shop sells old coins. I wonder if they could tell us something about the coin in your pendant." Kitty, who was wearing her gold coin necklace, entered the shop with David and showed the pendant to the owner of the shop. The expression on the shopkeeper's face changed like the passing shadow of a cloud on a partly sunny day as he remained intently engaged in examining the piece. He then made a quick phone call and asked Kitty, "Where did you get this?"

"It has been in our family for generations, what is it worth?"

A few moments passed as the shopkeeper further examined the coin without answering. An elderly man came into the shop and the shopkeeper thanked him for joining them and showed him the coin. The man took out his magnifying glass and examined the coin for quite some time. The whispering between the old man and the shopkeeper turned lively.

Finally Kitty broke their unending discussion with, "Signor, what do you make of the coin? Is it worth much?"

Both men looked up at Kitty and then the older one, slipping his magnifying glass into his inside jacket pocket, took a couple of steps closer to her and said, "Many factors determine the value of a gold coin, such as its rarity, age, condition and the number originally minted. Let me give you an example," he scratched his chin to further emphasize what he was about to disclose. "These are Portuguese. To be more precise, this is a 500 reais gold coin from the era of King Sebastian of Portugal. It dates back to the sixteenth century. It is worth quite a bit, if you are interested in selling it. What is your name, Signora?"

"Kitty, Kathleen Zuccato. No, we're not selling it," said Kitty and then asked, "it is an important part of our ancestry and it shall remain in our family forever, but would it be possible to find its worth? We have a pair of these."

The two men almost in unison responded, "A pair? Priceless." The older man turned to David as if the financial matters should only be discussed between men. "Signor, its true value could only be realized through an international auctioneer, perhaps Sotheby or Christie. You look like an Englishman. You understand what I am talking about? You cannot find a buyer for such rare coins here in Sienna. However, if you are interested, I have a cousin in Florence who would make you an offer, a generous one, I may add. He is a collector of historical buildings and artifacts. The Zuccato family is known in Florence and if you like, I could ask him to approach you there."

Both David and Kitty thanked the shopkeeper and the old man, indicating they were not interested in an offer and they left the shop. They said nothing further about the gold coin and made their way to the Ristorante La Pizzeria di nonno Mede where they had earlier agreed to meet with Mary for dinner. Mary was already waiting for them sipping a glass of wine. Kitty took charge of ordering and the evening turned out to be a gastronomic feast accompanied by a delicious bottle of Brunello di Montalcino from the famous Montalcino area.

After a long and sumptuous dinner, where David found Mary quite relaxed and enjoying his travel stories, they all drove back to the hotel where David took a separate room and bid them goodnight after thanking them for a wonderful evening. Lying in bed he thought of Mary, her attractive smile and the way she often laughed tonight. He considered himself lucky to have two such beautiful friends. Slowly he slipped into a luxurious sleep filled with amorous dreams.

25

As it turned out, in the next room to David, Mary was also sleeping alone. Kitty during the day had run into her old flame and after returning to the hotel after dinner, she told Mary all about it. Then she left her alone to spend the night and let her free spirit soar drinking and dancing all night long with her old friend. She also went to his apartment to spend the few remaining hours of an intoxicating night.

The next morning when David met Mary for breakfast, Kitty was missing. When asked about her absence, Mary with a slight frown explained, "She met up with someone so we will have to drive back together without her. Kitty and her friend will come to Florence later this evening. Is that awkward for you?"

"Awkward for me?" he asked, surprised, and quickly added, "not at all. I thought it might be awkward for you. I had told you that I would not get in your way and don't want to cause any trouble between you and Antonio, so would you like me to take the train back?"

She remained silent for a few moments. The longer her silence lasted, the longer she seemed unwilling to show her true feelings. Her silence gave encouragement to David that she may prefer his company but considered it inappropriate to admit. So to get her out of her dilemma, he offered, "I'd much rather travel back with you if it is no trouble to you. I won't mention it to anyone, as that is none of my business."

Mary looked at him with a face like that of a sad child that has lost his mom in a crowd and said, "I don't like to either hide anything from or lie about something to Antonio. But I won't abandon you. I will make an exception this one time and not say anything to Antonio, for he does not understand friendship. I would like you not to say anything to him either, please."

"Okay," said David and thought of using a little different tack to lighten up her mood, "but I've a condition."

"A condition?" she asked. "What condition?"

"We leave now and you show me the Tuscan countryside on our way back. Obviously we mustn't get back before Kitty does so let's take our time and arrive late this evening, hopefully coinciding with Kitty's arrival back at the car park in Florence."

"I never thought of that," she said contemplatively, "but I guess that is the way it is going to be. You drive a hard bargain."

"And there is another condition." David was enjoying this and liked the way Mary was responding, "I get to drive the car."

"It's a deal, but be careful, it is not my car, you understand?"

Hurriedly finishing breakfast, they checked out and with a suppressed smile, David sat behind the wheel and put the car in first gear, taking off as if first on the grid at the Formula One car race. Mary screamed and laughed at the same time at the sudden burst of speed and careless demeanor of David. She rolled down her window, undid her hair clip and let her hair fly in the wild rush of wind.

Listening to the loud music on the radio and feeling the fresh morning air on their faces, they arrived at San Gimignano. As they walked up its narrow cobblestone main street to the center of town, Mary explained, "This is my favorite place. It is just so beautiful."

"It is amazing," said David, looking around. "Aren't you going to give me a history lesson like Kitty does?"

"Only if you pay me like you pay Kitty," Mary was smiling and at the same time her cheeks were red. "Okay," she added, "because you asked so nicely, here it is." She cleared her throat and began, "San Gimignano was founded as a small village in the third century BC by the Etruscans. Historical records begin in the tenth century, when it adopted the name of the bishop Saint Geminianus, who had defended it from Attila's Huns."

"Ah, I beg to differ" David knew a little about this place and its confusing past, or perhaps he himself was confused, but interjected to tease Mary. "I know that San Gimignano is the birthplace of the thirteenth century poet Folgore da San Gimignano and the place is obviously named after him."

"Excuse me but it is my story so let me correct you." Mary seemed to warm to this banter, saying, "maybe the poet took his name from the town, did you ever think of that? This is a very old place. In the Middle Ages and Renaissance era, it was a stopping point for Catholic pilgrims on their way to Rome and the Vatican, as it sits on the medieval Via Francigena. In the twelfth century, during the period of its highest splendor, the city made itself independent from the bishops of Veltora and despite many hardships, somehow managed to embellish its artwork and architecture. But that is enough of history, let's go get some lunch."

"Oh, it is still early. Let's take a tour of the cathedral and then we will go to any restaurant of your choice." David was hankering for more history of the place and found the ambiance of this medieval city soothing. The tourist season was not in full swing yet so the quiet added mystery to the ancient structures.

"Okay," Mary returned, "but after the cathedral I must take you to my absolutely most favorite restaurant in Tuscany, it is called Il Trovatore—Pizzeria Ristorante San Gimignano. It is not far, it is on Via dei Fossi. The food cooked in a wood oven is to die for and the classical music they play is absolutely amazing."

As they entered the cathedral David felt a queer sensation. Overwhelmed by the sheer quantity and quality of the numerous fourteenth century frescoes, he thought they were nothing short of a picture book from medieval times telling stories of the old world. In the last row of benches he sat down and for a moment forgot that Mary was standing behind him, aware of nothing but comforting spirits hovering around him.

Mary stepped out of the cathedral, leaving him in his own world. He closed his eyes and leaned back against the bench. Inexplicable as it was, he felt the warmth in his soul to be a good omen, a notion, a cryptic message telling him that he was at the right place, not physically but spiritually. His breathing became deep and slow and it made him relax further; he was almost half asleep.

He opened his eyes and for a moment did not know where he was, but he felt rejuvenated. He stepped out and found Mary standing against a wall, and so joined her. "Sorry about that, Mary, I don't know what happened but I felt happy in there. Let's do that lunch, my treat."

"Please call me Maria, I prefer Maria," she smiled and together they made their way to the restaurant.

26

A romantic setting and delicious wine seemed to have brought David and Maria to a new level of trust in their fast growing friendship, all in the last twenty-four hours. Sitting opposite each other at a small, corner table in a quixotic restaurant of medieval ambiance and sipping on Giacomo Conterno, a Barolo produced in Italy's Piedmont region and derived from black Nebbiolo grape, for both it was a dreamy moment. Gazing into each other's eyes and without saying much, they seemed to have developed a language of their own, one that comes from the heart.

The interior of the restaurant was aglow with diffused light from a central chandelier and candlelight on tables created a dreamy ambience compared to the sunny day outside. Maria's hair cascading down one side of her shoulders and hypnotic eyes made her look as if an angel descended from the heavens. David wanted to know so much about her and, mellowed by the environment, boldly stated, "I know a very little about you. Would it be imprudent for me to ask who Maria Zuccato really is?"

Maria's eyes remained fixed on his face but her demeanor was as if she were trying to understand the sincerity of his question. David felt the awkwardness of her silence and quickly added, "I'm sorry. That was uncalled for."

A little twinkle in her eyes travelled down to her lips and broadened her smile as she finally responded, "No, you said nothing wrong. But to know Maria Zuccato, what she once was, you would first have to know Maria Giovanni, what I'm today. You think you have the time and patience for that?"

"I've all the time in the world for you and I would love to get to know both Marias. Who wouldn't? If you don't mind my saying, you're the most beautiful woman I have ever seen. We could be great friends, Maria, for we are very much alike and a little age difference, as you pointed out the other day, is of no consequence to me and shouldn't affect a wonderful partnership, I mean, friendship like this. Please, I have no hidden agenda, so let us both relax and get to know each other."

After prefacing her speech with, "I had dreams of being a successful woman in my own right," she began contemplatively, "when I was fifteen I read a lot about and was inspired by the story of Gabrielle 'Coco' Chanel. To me she is a state of mind and not just a fashion label. Ironically we both suffer from an unfair childhood. She lost her mother and, abandoned by her father, ended up being raised by an aunt and later in an orphanage. But she fought all that and created her own couture house that paved the way to women's liberation. Did you know that she was the first to feature a perfume named after a designer? As she liked to say, 'Fashion passes, style remains.' This was not your modern day woman, for she was born in 1883; she was way ahead of her time."

"Wow," David responded, raising his eyebrows, "she is quite a role model."

"She was a radical, a carefree revolutionary, and above all a visionary. She would not let traditional values hold her back. She even changed her name, her birth date, and her birthplace to continue to evolve into a fighting spirit. I loved what she said about ambition, 'How many cares one loses when one decides not to be something but to be someone.' "

"Maria," David asked, "it seems to me that you have spirit, beauty, sophistication, grace and are a great role model, so what is holding you back from becoming the Coco of the modern world?"

Maria picked up her wine glass and took a gulp as if to suppress some ugly feelings as she stared into her glass. Slowly she lifted her gaze to meet David's. There was an imperceptible look on her face as if she was in-between decisions, like deciding on something important. Finally she spoke, "I don't know you that well and you are still young, but maybe we have the chemistry that a friendship needs to be transparent. Let me share something with you, but please don't abandon me when you hear the truth?"

David waited and wondered what she had in mind. He had no notion of abandoning her no matter what the truth was. He had a strange sensation that whatever she was willing to share would only bring him closer to her. And he liked this feeling but could not help wondering if it was prudent for him to traverse down the path she was willing to go. Life, as he had known it thus far, was nothing but a complicated maze where without guidance he found himself helplessly lost. He knew he was vulnerable but he remained intrigued and looking into those deep blue eyes, said, "I would never abandon you and you know that. We are friends forever."

27

Mary lowered her gaze and, with the need to reveal her secrets to someone, realized she had been waiting for years to find a friend, a friend like David, who would listen to her story. Her secrets had been like a crushing stone on her soul beneath which her spirit had been gradually withering. Though she was afraid that there was a chance, no matter how remote, that sharing her intimate and dark secrets may drive David away, in her heart of hearts she felt that the right moment had come for her to take a chance.

Perhaps David was not yet quite comfortable enough to open up his secrets to her but she remained convinced that he, like her, had a tumultuous past and maybe destiny had brought them together to ease each other's pain. If she had understood David well then there was a strong possibility that the mutual sharing of secrets may bring them close as friends, and perhaps even as soul mates.

"I was raped when I was seventeen," her voice quivered as her emotions choked her.

David's eyes widened as if trying to visualize the terror of a seventeen-year-old girl being raped. David asked, "Have you not been able to discuss this with Antonio? Are you afraid that he might somehow hold you responsible for it?" He looked intently at her and added, "Maria, you must not keep it a secret from Antonio. He may be a sentimental Italian man but he may surprise you by his compassion. Confiding in him may release you from this burden and together you can find a way forward."

"Stop!" she cried. "Stop it, David. It is Antonio who raped me. He is the last person who would understand my hurt and my torture."

"I'm so sorry, Maria," David responded. "Tell me, please, tell me how did it all happen?"

"It was our wedding night," she said in a reflective voice, her face contorted in a grimace. "I remember vaguely Antonio coming into my bedroom and bolting the door behind him. His eyes were wild and he looked intoxicated with his conquest. He looked as if the animal within him had arisen and the dark side of his personality possessed him. I was too scared and stunned to resist his advances and too young to understand the calamity that was about to befall. I kept thinking that this nightmare could not be the sanctified gift of heaven the padre at the church spoke of in the afternoon."

Mary paused to blink away tears. Her grimace dissolved into determination. "My eyes were closed, an eddying darkness seemed to swim 'round me, and reflections of my childhood came in as black and confused. Self-abandoned and defeated, I seemed to lie on the darkened ground of a great forest. I heard a roar of crackling fire carried on the wings of a wild wind in the surrounding mountains, and felt the scorching heat come. I had no will to flee; I had no strength. I lay faint, longing to be dead."

"Oh Maria, I'm so sorry," David, in absence of any other suitable words of comfort, repeated himself. "It must be so cruel and unjust for you?"

Mary nodded. "One idea only still throbbed life-like somewhere deep within me—a remembrance of the Virgin Mary: It precipitated an unuttered prayer. These words played in my mind as something that should be whispered, but no strength came to bring them to my lips—'Do not drift away from me, child, for the devil is near. You have been betrayed and there is none to help.' The devil was near, he was upon me, and I had raised no entreaty to Madonna to obviate it, as I had not joined my hands in supplication, nor bent down on my knees in prayer, nor moved my lips to call upon Her. The devil came: In full fury of burning fire, he swept through me, mercilessly ravaging my body and my soul."

Almost in a monotone, she continued, "The whole consciousness of my life was forsaken, my love vanished, my hope quenched, my faith death-struck. That bitter hour of my life cannot be described. In truth, fire came into my soul. I sank deep in a pile of hot ashes; like smoldering ember I felt the breath of death in my face. I felt nothing but scorched earth around me, the fire had reduced me to an insignificant nothing. I was a woman burning in the fires of hell of traditional values created by men."

As Mary disclosed the horrors of her wedding night, finally the gravity of its terror struck a chord in David's heart. He remembered the age difference between Mary and Antonio and for the first time understood its ugly significance. Thirty-one years old, Antonio knew exactly what he was doing to a seventeen-year-old young and innocent girl and there was only one word that could appropriately describe it and its horrors—rape. His jaw clenched and his dislike for Antonio turned into a hatred.

Mary, reliving the dread of her wedding night, continued, "But, then, faint as it was, a voice within me averred that I could do it and foretold that I should do it. It was the woman in me vowing not to let die the girl in me. I wrestled with my own resolution: I wanted to be strong that I might avoid the awful passage of further suffering I saw laid out for me, and then suddenly I felt the presence of the Madonna, weeping. In her sorrow for my suffering, I vowed to fight tyranny, promised to find passion, and told myself that with Her by my side, I would salvage my soul from the unsounded depths of agony."

Mary paused and then fell into silence. Suddenly David turned away with an indecipherable exclamation, full of a rising emotion that frightened him. He stood up and walked a few steps away from the table then came back. He stooped down and held her hands in his as if to kiss them but he remembered caresses were forbidden for she was a married woman.

He looked into her eyes and said, "I understand that you are bound by the values laid out by society and its age-old customs and traditions, but how could you face that man, that animal every day in your house, the one who so monstrously snatched love and innocence from you when you were only seventeen?" David kept his voice low and soft for he did not want to sound as if he was blaming her. He affirmed, "Laws about morality and integrity for a man are not for the times when there is no temptation, they are for such moments as what you just described, when body and soul rise in mutiny against their rigor, severe are they, intangible they shall not be. If a man at his individual convenience might break them, what would be their worth? What would be his worth? Leave him. Find a way to get him out of your life."

A pause. "Why are you silent, Maria?"

"You're not of Catholic faith, the one my family brought me up in. You don't know what you are saying. You condemn me to live wretched and to die accursed?" Her voice rose. "I would have you know that no matter how harsh, I will live sinless for I wish to die tranquil. You hide it well but I know your pain. We are not so different, we were born to strive and endure—you and I. So do so."

David, though he hated when people hid behind religion and as a result let the guilty go unpunished, felt it was neither the time nor the place to push Maria too hard. She was looking frail and vulnerable and he let the silence between them console her.

28

After that period of silence they had begun to talk in soft voices but not about Mary's wedding night. They talked about the beauty of Tuscany and about the future. David shared his ambition to write a book one day but included that he still was struggling to find the right subject to inspire him. Suddenly David looked at his watch and exclaimed, "Oh my god," he tapped his wristwatch with his index finger, "do you realize what time it is?"

Maria, with a sharp intake of breath, cried, "Oh, no. Kitty will not have the wisdom to wait for me in the car park and instead she will arrive at the house before me. We agreed to meet in the car park where we picked you up, by the crossroads at five so we could go to the house together and it is five now. We still have an hour's drive ahead of us. I hope she has the sense to wait for me and not barge into our home on her own."

David clasped his head in both his hands and said, "I'm so sorry, Maria, but I had no idea it was so late. And did you realize that we have had the whole bottle of wine? I feel a little tipsy, don't you? Anyway, let's get going. I'll drive you back as fast as I can. Let's hope Kitty waited for us."

They quickly settled the bill and stepped out of the restaurant but were hit with tiny droplets of rain. The bright sunny summer day had become casualty to heavy overcast skies with threatening storm clouds gathering overhead. This was so uncharacteristic of summer weather but at times the arrival of warm days carrying moist air in their wake brought unsettled and windy weather. It had become prematurely dark and strong winds started to whip from the north to sweep through the entire Tuscan valley. David took his linen jacket off and put it around Mary's shoulders to give her some protection from the rain as they made a dash for the car.

"We cannot go too fast in such weather, the roads will be too slippery," David warned and sitting close behind the wheel, leaned in to the windshield to squint up at the sky in hopes of finding a break in the clouds. But just then a bolt of lightning tore the sky in half and with a loud crack, thunder struck somewhere on the hills not too far away. Mary let out a little scream and tightly grabbed David's arm with both hands, saying, "I hate being out in the storm. Let's head for Florence."

David started the engine and eased the car out of the parking lot and onto the road. Thunderous, jagged lightning was now repeatedly striking the Tuscan valley with vengeance and lighting up the dark day with its blinding glare. The rain started to gather strength and sheets of it were now coming from every direction. David turned the wipers on at full speed but through the downpour like a river on the windshield, could only see blurry images of road and trees. David managed to drive a few kilometers under such treacherous conditions and then saw the sign of Hotel Vecchio Asilo that was located in a nearby village of Ulignano and he turned the car in that direction.

"What are you doing, David?" Maria asked him. "You're going the wrong way."

"Listen," David shouted to be heard over the wind and rain, "it's downright suicidal to drive in these conditions. I cannot see a thing out there and we both had a little too much to drink. God forbid, but if we get involved in an accident then we would have a lot of explaining to do to your family and especially to Antonio. God knows, we might get killed out here. I cannot endanger your life. We will be better off stopping here in the hotel till this passes over. Summer storms often don't last long."

"Oh, god," she cried, "I should have never listened to Kitty in the first place. This is a disaster." David drove to the entrance of the hotel, let Maria out and then parked the car. They both sat in the lobby and the owner, after listening to their predicament, brought them hot coffee and a plateful of biscotti, urging them to stay as long as they wanted.

An hour passed and then another and there was no letting up in the weather. The owner reappeared with some fresh coffee and in a friendly tone said, "This weather is amazing. In the forty years I have been here, I have never seen rain like this, in the summer. The roads will be flooded by now. I'm afraid you may not be able to drive tonight in these conditions so you may want to consider staying overnight. Think about it, and let me know if I can help."

After the owner of the hotel disappeared somewhere in the back room, David looked at Maria, whose anxiety for some reason seemed to be waning, and said, "We have no other option but to spend the night here. I will book two separate rooms, of course, and let me talk to Antonio tomorrow. I'll explain to him how we were trapped by the weather. He could talk to the hotel owner here. He may be angry about us spending the night here but hey, we have done nothing wrong and our consciences are clear."

Mary smiled for the first time in the past hour and she had a look in her eyes that David had not seen before. It was as if she had won a little battle or maybe she had a taste of freedom and that was why she looked elated. She threw her head back and stuck her chin out defiantly, responding, "Yes, you are right, David. I'm not afraid of Antonio, I was just worried that Kitty may feed him some stupid story about me not turning up tonight and she would then be embarrassed when the truth comes out. Anyway, we'll face that tomorrow."

David went over to the reception and rang the bell and when the owner appeared, talked with him and managed to get keys for two separate but adjoining rooms. A few minutes later they checked in and retired to their respective rooms to rest for a while and freshen up. They agreed to meet again in two hours for dinner downstairs.

29

Maria lay in her bed but rather than worrying what Antonio would say tomorrow, she wondered about what David was thinking next door. She stared at the door that separated their rooms. How easy it would be to knock on that door and invite David in for company. What would he think of such an offer, she wondered? He would think exactly what she had been thinking. She smiled.

She began to understand what David meant to her. Freedom. The beautiful pure freedom of a woman was infinitely more wonderful than any sexual love and David through his unselfish companionship was offering her a taste of that freedom. But did he derive the same pleasure from it as she did? The unfortunate truth was that men lagged so far behind women in this matter. A woman could yield to a man by baring her inner self without yielding her physical self. Did he feel what she did right now?

After a brief moment she let out a big sigh and chastised herself for having such thoughts. It must be the wine and she knew that rain always excited her. As she closed her eyes for a little nap she realized that she was falling for David and with a pang of sadness, she also realized that nothing good would ever come of it. She could never have him. David was young and perhaps in love with Kitty and she was older than he and married. She turned over on her stomach and buried her face in the pillow. *Why?* Between sobs she whispered again, *why?*

At seven in the evening Maria came down looking fresh and stunning as always. David was sitting in a sofa chair by the fire that the owner had lit to warm up the place, and was sipping on red wine with an open bottle and an empty glass on the table in front of him. Mary sat opposite him in a matching sofa chair and asked, "Are you planning on becoming an alcoholic?"

David smiled and pouring a little wine in her glass, answered, "No, because we are going to share this bottle. But I must say I am developing a real taste for Tuscan wines. This is Vino Nobile di Montepulcioano and like Brunello di Montalcino, it too is made from Sangiovese grapes."

"You're becoming quite an expert on our wines," Mary said warmly as she picked up her glass.

"A little help from the hotel owner; it is his recommendation." David, encouraged by her smile and relaxed demeanor, despite the threat of serious confrontation with Antonio, now said something that even surprised him. The words were out of his mouth before his mind could check them. "God took extra time in making you. Here is to the most beautiful lady I have ever met."

As they clinked their glasses, Mary blushed, responding, "Do you flirt like this with everyone?"

"No," he said with a grin, enjoying the moment, "just with one."

"Please, don't start. I know you are a very sweet man but I am not sure mixing all this wine and flirting is a good idea." Her sudden subdued look startled David, for he did not want to hurt her. He pursed his lips. "What shall we talk about then?" he asked, resorting to joviality to lighten up her mood.

"I opened up my heart to you earlier at lunch time, why don't you tell me who the real David Hawthorne is?"

"To tell you about the real David Hawthorne, I must tell you about Mr. Hawthorne, my father."

"I'm listening." Mary placed her wine glass down on the table and fixed her gaze on him.

David moved close to the edge of his chair. "My father personifies the nation's pride, its arrogance, its honor and in it, its folly. Nothing but the military matters to my dad, and he is a man of men. He believes that fighting for freedom is a man's natural instinct and there is nothing nobler than to be a military man. His emphasis was not always as much on freedom as it was on fighting. And he believed that, for the risks he took, he deserved to live life on the edge—drinking, gambling and chasing women. My mother gave up her dreams and hopes for him and he broke her heart. Broken confidences can be mended, but there is no glue in the world that can mend a broken heart. A heart doesn't crash, it simply folds like a lone wave ebbs out in an open ocean, unnoticed, unheard and inconsequential. But he was and is blinded by the military code of living on the edge; family and their needs come afterwards."

"Oh, I'm so sorry, David," she said, touching his hands. "I didn't know you had such a difficult time with your dad. I thought you two were pals for Kitty told me that you too are a military man."

"Was, I was a military man, but that is all behind me now." His voice was low and tone contemplative, raising his voice might make old memories come alive. He let out a sigh, finding release in the comfort of sharing. "Winds of war never die down; they simply shift through time and across the globe. What has senseless killing accomplished? It is not freedom from oppression or right to self-rule, these are the reasons given, but behind it is nothing but control of trade and commerce by those who are already powerful. They are the ones with their finger on the trigger. And the soldier must spend the rest of his life with blood on his conscience. No, I am done with all this. No more soldiering, not for me."

30

The thunder had ceased outside, but the rain, which had abated, suddenly came down with a last blast of lightning and a mutter of the departing storm. Mary was ecstatic that he had talked for so long, as it seemed he was really talking to himself, not to her. Melancholy seemed to envelop him completely, and she realized that she was getting closer to him as he opened up to her. She knew once she had won his confidence she would have a soul mate. And she enjoyed the triumph. She opened the door and stared at the straight heavy rain, like a steel curtain, with a sudden desire to rush out into it, to sing and dance. Finally the rain abated. There was a wet, heavy, perfumed stillness. Evening was approaching.

Though they would spend the night in separate rooms, sleeping next door to each other was exciting. Even in their serious discussion, now and then a flicker of a smile would dance on their lips. During dinner they spoke of the injustice in their lives. The openness with which they spoke brought them closer. Often David thought of caressing Maria's hands that were placed on the table between them, but was not sure if that was what Maria wanted. Desire was stirring romantic feelings in his heart.

Candlelight and soft music accompanied dinner and as they sipped on espresso, the time finally came to go to their rooms. While they dragged the evening out just to be in each other's company, they maintained distance so as not to cross the boundary of no return. Finally and reluctantly Maria looked at her watch and suggested that they better retire so as to have an early start the next day.

At her door they both paused momentarily and then David leaned forward and in customary European style kissed her softly on both her cheeks. As David stepped back he noticed her dark eyelashes resting on her pink cheeks. Her ruby red lips stirred a sense of ecstasy in his heart and just for a moment he had a desire to kiss her lips. Suddenly she opened her eyes and with a smile of victory she stepped back towards the door. As they entered their respective rooms they saw the owner had opened the interconnecting door and it was Maria who spoke, "Close the door...." As he swung the door softly shut, the music seemed quivering just outside.

They both lay in their beds behind closed doors and with open hearts. Hearts that were longing for what they had not had for a long, long time—a caring touch, and love. It seemed that they both had developed tender feelings for each other but were afraid to disclose them for fear of being misunderstood. *He is the friend I always wanted*, she would contemplate, while David would wonder if she could be the love he had been yearning for. Mercifully and finally a heavy sleep descended on both and their amorous feelings turned their dreams into a world of desire and exhilaration.

The next morning at dawn, the sun tested and teased the horizon with its silvery perimeter then gradually filled the eastern sky with its golden glow. The morning was calm as if the storm of the previous day never happened.

David never expected that he would wake up feeling like this. He remembered every detail of the previous day and he knew that a perfectly novel experience had befallen him unlike anything he had known before. At the same time he recognized clearly that the dream that had fired his imagination was hopelessly unattainable—so that he felt positively ashamed of it, and he hastened to pass to the other more practical cares and difficulties bequeathed him by that blessed yesterday.

At Maria's insistence they had a quick breakfast of croissant and cappuccino and with Maria now behind the wheel they set off for Florence. David asked, "Did you sleep well?"

"Yes, thank you. And you?"

"Yeah, fine," he responded. Then, with a shake of his head, he said in a polite but firm voice, "Look, if you need me to explain, you know, to Antonio about the circumstance that kept us from returning yesterday, then please let me know, won't you? I don't want you to be in trouble on my account."

"You ought to quit worrying so much about Antonio. I'm not afraid of him. I am no longer a child and can manage quite well on my own," Maria responded with a thin smile and firm voice.

David let a moment of silence pass between them and then inquired, "Could I ask you something?"

"What is bothering you, David?" Maria gave him a quick side-glance and then, turning her attention back to the road, said, "Fire away. I had a feeling you would find a way to ask about what is troubling you."

"You don't have to answer if you don't want but do you hate your husband for what he did to you?"

"Hating him would be too easy. We haven't slept together since the horrible wedding night. Oh, he was ashamed the following morning for what he did, as if that could make it right. Anyway, he has agreed to wait until such time that I feel I am ready for him. But I've chosen as a just resolution to be indifferent till he understands the gravity of his heinous act and apologizes to me from his heart." Maria's voice was low and soft but there was an undertone of firm determination.

"What could be done to offer justice for what he did? And you think then that one day he will become a good and loving husband and you will spend your life with him happily ever after? Do you really think that his waiting for you is an act of forgiveness?"

Maria gave a soft laugh and said, as she shook her head, "You men do think on a different wavelength than we women. Justice will be done when he realizes that the right thing for him is to find a way to let me go. There is no other reasonable response to what he did, knowingly or unknowingly. He must release me." Her voice suddenly became stern, as did the expression on her face.

"I understand that this is the just punishment for him." David responded, although he realized that lost faith couldn't be regained through forgiveness.

"I'm not doing anything to punish him. It is neither punishment nor an act of revenge; it is simply an attempt to put the clock back to the time when Antonio and I were strangers. And before you translate this explanation into some way of starting fresh with Antonio, it is not. Okay? It is starting all over again for me, just me. I want to go back to the time when I was living an unencumbered life and this can only happen when I am alone again or with someone whom I choose."

She looked exhausted but also relieved, as if a heavy burden had been lifted off her soul. As if she wanted David to know who she really was, not a picture-perfect beauty but a human being, recognized for her attributes. She seemed comfortable sharing her feelings with him and he hoped this would lead to her becoming what he craved: a true friend at last.

31

Swinging the car sharply into the car park where she had picked up David the day before, Mary noticed the car park was empty except for a small blue vehicle in a corner of the lot. She parked as far from the blue car as possible to avoid detection in case it was someone who knew her, and asked David to leave her there so she could walk back to her house. But there was always a chance that Kitty had not yet made it to the house and was waiting somewhere for Maria to turn up.

Suddenly the car that was parked roared toward them and as it came to a screeching halt, Kitty jumped out and raced over to Maria, waving her arms. In an excited voice she shouted, "I was hoping you would come in the morning because I was sure you were held up by the storm. I too arrived about ten minutes ago, and this is my friend." She introduced a rather muscle-bound man who resembled a soccer star. Both Mary and David let out a sigh of relief and David stepped out of the car as Kitty jumped in and addressed David, "I am so sorry to have abandoned you, but I will make it up to you when we get together tomorrow. Is tomorrow morning at nine okay?" David nodded in the affirmative and they drove off in a hurry while Kitty's friend offered David a ride back to his hotel.

Upon the women's arrival at the house, Grandma thanked them for looking after her friend and neither sister had to explain about the storm and how they were held up by it for Grandma and Antonio assumed that they stayed an extra day to provide good care to the sickly neighbor. There was a silent understanding between the sisters to keep their mouths shut as Maria returned to her bedroom and Kitty went out, both without asking the other about how they spent the night.

Maria watered the fern plants on the windowsill and then sat by the open window sipping a hot cup of coffee. The events of yesterday were flitting around in her head. She found it hard to hold onto any thought except this strange feeling of elation as well as a sweet pang at missing David, wondering when she would be able to see him again. Yesterday's experience had made her bolder and she was now willing to take risks, but as soon as the thought lifted her spirits, the stern face of Grandma and frowning face of Antonio also floated into her mind.

Like an ocean, deep yet calm on the surface, she could see into David's soul, knowing that he was the same as her, the same as the ocean. She did not like raging rivers for no matter how powerful, how deep, how long such rivers might be, they remain destined to diminish their existence without a trace into the depths of the ocean.

She wondered why thinking of David caused such a stir in her. She adored and hated him at the same time for he made her suffer. She wanted him to go away and as soon as such a thought occurred she yearned for him to stay where he was, in her heart. Suddenly a thought struck and she gasped, with a sharp intake of breath. *Is this what they call love?* she wondered. The sweet pain of missing someone, wanting to throw all caution to the wind, she had not known such feelings before. "Oh Lord," she whispered, "thank you for bringing love into my life, but now please bring us happiness."

She wanted to go out and find David and yearned to confess her love to him but expressing love to your beloved is not easy, for even Cupid needs the help of a bow and an arrow. She could only hope that the tides of time would be in her favor and evoke similar feelings in David. In the sea of hope, she cast her fortune with the outgoing tide and was willing to let the sea decide the course of her fate, for she had learned to appreciate that life is nothing without adventure.

She had believed that the answer to the riddle of happiness lay in the simplicity of life and in the complexity of its philosophy. And she knew that something had to change for she had failed to decipher what was happening to her life. She never could figure out the emotional chicken-and-egg conundrum—was she unhappy because she was depressed or was she depressed because she was unhappy. She decided that later she would go out to the café where David took his meals and maybe spend a few minutes with him over a cup of coffee. She drifted into a daydream of what would they talk about when they met again.

Upon returning to his room, David dropped his luggage and went out for some air. He moved from alley to alley. He sat down in a chair in a piazza and then changed to another chair, after which he walked about again, only again to repeat both actions. His eagerness to see Mary again was apparent in his excited state of mind as he pointlessly wandered the streets.

Finally he chose a new restaurant where he had not eaten before and ordered a glass of Chianti and Linguini with white clam sauce. As he sat sipping chilled white wine, he remembered what his mother had once told him, 'You cannot second-guess life, you have to live it.' *But isn't life with Maria a dream?* he wondered. *Is it unattainable, for she is married and bound by her rigid Catholic values?* He knew that he should do the right thing by not pursuing the path that obviously led to disaster, but strong feelings of desire were weakening his sense of prudence.

His was a tortured elation by wanting to believe in the fulfillment of his desires and then at the same very moment the reality came that spelled danger.

Later that evening Maria, dressed up in a dark mauve dress with a matching silk scarf and black high-heel shoes, left her house on the pretence of finding Kitty for she had not returned the whole day. Antonio usually came late around dinnertime and Grandma never questioned the movements of the two sisters.

As Maria stepped out of her house, she decided that there are times in life when one asks endless questions and one is left bewildered by the injustice of unfair deeds, but then there are times in life like this that offer all the answers one has been craving. *It is all so clear to me now. There is finally a purpose in what I do, what I am about to do.* And then with determination, she headed towards the restaurant where she hoped to find David.

32

David's heart missed a beat as he saw Maria like a goddess descending from heaven enter the restaurant and approach his table. Without hesitation, David leaned forward and kissed her on both cheeks and this time lingered just that extra moment for his lips to feel the softness and velvety texture of her skin. Lorenzo smiled at them and pulled a chair out for Maria to take a seat opposite David in a quiet corner where they could talk in privacy.

"I don't know what is happening to us, David," she began, "but I had to come and see you. God knows I love seeing you and spending time in your company." She paused momentarily as if seeking control over her emotions, but she further added, "I think we are crossing a boundary, which may lead to temptation. I don't think I can handle it, I think we ought to stop seeing each other. Our objectives maybe the same but our paths are different."

David for a moment thought that he had misheard her. He could understand that she was afraid and in a difficult situation but he did not expect things to come to halt so abruptly. David chose his words carefully so as not to escalate her fear when he said, "Don't run from what you have been seeking. Life is not a beautiful thing on its own. It is the gifted, caring and passionate people who make life beautiful. Conversely, uncaring, hateful and vengeful people can make life unbearable. What I am trying to say is that one life is not equal to another, as life is not inherently fair. Choose your path carefully if you want to see the light. I am not asking you to promise anything, just let us be friends."

"I'm not lost in darkness," she said, fixing her wide blue eyes on his face. "I'm merely standing in the shadows. See, there is a difference, for where I am now I know that seeing the light is merely a matter of time. I am as certain of shadows dissipating with the passing of night as you are certain that light will emerge with the rising sun. I am living a promise I never made. I do not know how to explain it to you."

David sat in silence for several moments. He neither spoke nor moved.

"I see myself on an unbounded sea, on its breast as a ship starting, spreading all sails, effortlessly moving across its vast expanse. My heart like its pennant is flying aloft as she speeds—below waves press forward that surround the ship with motion. I feel free as a bird soaring high on the rising mountain winds. And I owe all this to your friendship, you have shown me the path to freedom, but our paths remain divergent for many reasons."

"But why," cried David and involuntarily cupped her hands that were playing with a flower on the table. She did not object to him holding her hands. "As you say, we are friends, and our friendship must not be tarnished because of fear of our crossing the boundary you talked about, for I shall never take advantage of our friendship."

"We must stop seeing each other. This is our goodbye." She released her hands from David's to fight tears that welled up in her eyes.

David felt as if an earthquake had rolled under his feet. Maintaining his gaze on her, he asked, "Goodbye?"

Hoping to change her mind and break the severity of silence, David spoke again. "I thought we were close friends. Friends help each other, especially in time of need. We have opened our hearts to each other. I have never told things I have told you and I am glad I did. You think that you can forget about me? You do not feel a special bond between us?"

David's voice wavered as something stirred in his heart and he felt he was pleading rather than complaining.

Maria closed her eyes and two tiny tears rolled down her cheeks as she in an almost inaudible voice said, "You haven't shared much with me about your past, not like what I told you of mine. But anyway, it is not about that. I assure you that you will forget me before I forget you. You are very dear to me."

Half of heaven in the golden hue of subdued dusk was pure and stainless. The clouds, now fleeing before the wind, had shifted to the west, filing off eastward in long, golden plumes. The people in the restaurant were engaged in their various animated discussions, indifferent to his seismic changes within.

He was silent despite the black void of despair inside. That was the death of all desire, the death of all love. David sat stunned, looking at her back as she walked away from the table, away from him and out of his life. "Farewell," was the cry of his heart as she left him. Despair added, "Farewell forever."

33

Maria went home realizing the depth of her feelings toward David. Although she said goodbye, those feelings were still alive in her, and with all her heart she still adored him. She adored him till her knees were weak. She hoped that having said goodbye she would feel liberated and unencumbered but somehow she felt the opposite, and closer to David than ever before.

She was alive with yearning for him, vulnerable and helpless in adoration of him. She said to herself, *I feel like a young and innocent girl.* And so she did, as if her heart that had been shut for years had opened and filled with new life, almost a burden, yet lovely.

It was not the passion that was new to her. It was the yearning adoration. She knew she had always wanted yet feared it, for it left her helpless. She feared it still, lest if she adored him too much, then she would lose herself, become effaced, and she did not want to be a dependent, like a housewife. She had a devil of self-will in her breast. Could she allow in the love to grow, she wondered, and then answered herself quietly, yes, she could follow her passion if she wanted, but denying it was not a weakness on her part, for it made her stronger.

So, in the flux of new awakening, the old hard passion flamed in her for a time and she checked it. She felt the force of her renewed confidence in her limbs, the woman within her gleaming, beating down the male domination of the old Italian world, but her heart was heavy.

She was walking away from what she always wanted and she knew it. She did not want it now, though, at least not until such time as all injustices in her life were eliminated or justly punished, and till that time the adoration was her treasure. This feeling was so fathomless, so deep and so unknown. No, no, she would give up her hard bright womanpower; she would sink into the voiceless song of adoration. It was early yet to seek liberation from her husband but that is what she must do if she wanted David.

She had a peculiar, childish wistfulness at times, and this not only confounded David, with this an intangible aloofness pierced his heart. It seemed to David he should never know her. Only a day before, she was so open, revealing her darkest secrets, and today she had simply walked away. He remained sitting where she had left him with his mind in a whirl.

It was as if she would sacrifice a relationship with him rather than renounce her age-old, religious values or seek ways to get rid of her husband. There was something in her that David could never understand, so that never, never could he say he was a friend of hers or she was of his. There was a strange closeness and yet an inexplicable distance between them but now it seemed it was all over. She wanted it to be over and he was too much of a gentleman not to grant her wishes. Where should he go from here? he wondered. The love he had found, he lost before he could even claim it.

Lorenzo watching Maria leave abruptly came to David's table. David apologized for the disruption and paying a hefty tip to Lorenzo, asked him to cancel the dinner. Before Lorenzo could speak, David left the restaurant. Even though in his mind he knew it was wrong, involuntarily his feet carried him towards Maria's house. The closer he got to her house the faster his heart raced. He did not know what he would do when he reached her house. Then he was standing across the road from her home. As if awakening from a daydream, suddenly he realized where he was and hurriedly looked around as if afraid of being caught doing something inappropriate, and so quickly moved away.

He wandered the streets absentmindedly with the utter loneliness one often has in a crowd of strangers. He kept circling around her house as if drawn by some enigmatic force. Fifty yards away from her house he noticed a bar and went in. He wanted some comfort and against his best judgment decided to seek it in a drink. It seemed a local joint for there were no tourists in this family-run small bar and a few groups of locals were drinking heavily. He ordered a glass of wine and then changed his mind and asked for beer.

As the heavyset waiter with apron tied around his girth and a napkin thrown over his shoulder put a glassful of beer in front of David, he picked it up and gulped it down with relish, as though quenching a flame in his breast. But in another minute the beer had gone to his head, and a faint and even pleasant shiver ran down his spine. He asked for another. His sense of loneliness and incoherent thoughts grew more disconnected, and as soon as he finished the second glass of beer a light, pleasant drowsiness came upon him. He requested one more and the waiter, with a little shake of his head, as if offering a polite warning, brought another glass. With a sense of comfort he rested his head against the wall, sighed softly and sank into a deep, sound, melancholy mood. Despite his outer calm, he was raging inside at losing Maria's friendship and, afraid of his own power, he vowed to remain in the bar and cool off. Under his breath he cursed Antonio, who had taken away the little happiness that David truly believed was his.

Taking small sips now and then from his third glass of beer, he felt some comfort and began to scan the place. About five yards away and directly in front of him were three large men sitting with their backs to him. They were talking in low voices that he could not hear clearly over the background music, but every now and then the two men on either side of the middle person would turn to look at David and laugh. David thought it odd and considered approaching them to ask what was so funny. The beer was playing games with his head and a suppressed rage deep in his heart was dancing on the periphery of prudence. Finally he shook his head as if evoking judiciousness and he decided to ignore them. Their laughter became louder and though David maintained his composure, it became increasingly disconcerting to him. Then suddenly something happened that he had not expected. The man in the middle turned his head to look over his shoulder and gave a derisive smile.

It was Antonio.

34

A sharp feeling of hatred rose from the pit of David's stomach like an acid and he had a bitter taste in his mouth. Neither said anything except stared at the other, unblinking. Antonio's eyes were dilated and he looked drunk. David's jaw clenched and his grip tightened around his beer glass.

Antonio was in his evening clothes as if he was dressed to go out for dinner or a party. He wore a light grey fashionable loose coat, light summer trousers, and everything about him was loose, fashionable and spick and span; his linen, irreproachable. His gold watch was massive, matching a large gold ring on his finger. On the same wrist where he wore his gold watch, he had the bracelet that Maria had given him and he was stroking the pendant as if it was a living thing. In his manner he was nonchalant, and at the same time studiously free and easy; he made no effort to conceal his self-importance.

His two friends were fat men, puffy, colorless, with clean-shaven faces and straight, flaxen hair. Their resemblance to each other gave an uncanny impression as of twins. Antonio continued to stare at David and there was a smile on his lips, and a new shade of irritable impatience was apparent in that smile.

David felt infuriated and his spleen rose within him. He almost choked with rage at himself as soon as he felt that strange desire to have a fight with Antonio; he wanted to punish him for what he did and was doing to Maria. He knew that he could take all three men on, for his combat training and rigorous military exercises had taught him how to neutralize the enemy, even if that meant killing them. Killing them was a thought that smoldered like a glowing ember in his mind. "You are either mad, or...," he muttered, stunned by the idea that had suddenly flashed into his mind.

Suddenly Antonio stopped smiling, stood up and with two big men on either side, walked up to David. David was strong and muscled, a trained military man, and could not be brought down easily.

As Antonio stood in front of David, in-between them was a heavy, dark oak table. David noticed that Antonio's face was flushed with excessive drinking; his eyes with a wild look in them were seeking a challenge. The full red lower lip projected a little as did his chin, and this irregularity gave his face a menacing expression. It was David who spoke first. "I've no fight with you. Don't even think of doing something stupid or I will teach you a lesson that you and your friends won't forget."

David saw the man's lower lip quiver with indignation at his insolent, harsh and challenging words—and his fate was sealed. Antonio stood as though lost in thought, and a strange, disdainful, half senseless grin strayed over his lips. David watched him closely, prepared for any sudden move from Antonio and his burley friends. Suddenly he remembered the Falklands and felt as if he was being ambushed again. What if any of the three men had a concealed weapon? Dark alarming ideas rose in his mind; the idea that he was in an ambush and at that moment he must use all force necessary in self-defense was increasing, leaving the realm of reason, that he ought perhaps to be doing something different from what he was now.

As Antonio spoke, the smile on his lips froze: apparently a spasm caught his breath. "David," he said, grinding his teeth, in the tone one might fancy of a speaking automaton to announce its single word. "David," he reiterated, and he went over the syllable three times, growling and in the intervals of speaking, shaking with burning fury. He hardly seemed to know what he was doing.

David's mind pulling on his judiciousness was advising him not to let this situation escalate but deep in his heart he was aching for Antonio to make the first move. Fighting his mixed feelings and thinking of Mary, David in a calm voice spoke, "Maria and I are just friends like I am friends with Kitty. Maria is a person of faith and she will tell you the same as I am telling you now."

Antonio took a deep breath as if drawing strength to have a showdown. "So it is Maria now, is it? It's like your impudence to say so. I expected it of you; I heard it in your voice the first time we spoke."

"Did you? You've a quick ear," said David, watching carefully the two fat friends on either side of Antonio.

"I have, and a quick eye and a quick brain. I know what is going on, don't take me for a fool."

"You need those faculties to survive these useless friends that are feeding you gossip."

"I do, especially when I've Mary's friends like you to deal with."

David was keeping a watchful eye on all three, when an unexpected incident broke the thread of his musings.

Two more people, large and muscle-bound, entered the bar and shouted Antonio's name. He turned briefly and gestured for them to come to him. With a swagger they came and stood behind the two friends that were already there. They were now five.

David realized the odds were stacking up against him but his courage did not waver. He did wonder, though, how far Antonio would go playing his stupid games to get rid of David. Games like he played with Maria's family. Antonio had married Maria by using his financial muscle and exploiting her father's unfortunate obsession. David wondered if Antonio perhaps was responsible for fuelling the gambling mania in Maria's father because it suited him, for he knew all along that one day he could manipulate their family situation to his advantage. But one thing he knew now for sure, and that generated a curious feeling in his heart: that she had not given him her love, and that his qualifications were ill-adapted to win from her that treasure. This was the point—this was where the nerve was touched and teased—this was where the fever was sustained and fed. He could not charm her. David felt convinced that she could never belong to Antonio for he had already lost her the day he thought he had won her, their wedding day. It was this rejection, David thought, that was behind Antonio's game in trying to intimidate David. He did not know David and his incalculable strength and fighting skills.

Antonio stood still and gazed at David, as though measuring his strength. At last Antonio's face changed. Seeming satisfied that David was frightened by his threat he assumed a harsh and unfriendly air. It produced an indescribable effect on David. His hatred for Antonio started to surge again.

Antonio's lips were twisted in a condescending smile, but he was in no conciliatory mood. He spoke rather loud, and was obviously consumed by his excitement, but David only wanted to smash his face in for all the cruelty he had shown toward Maria.

"You could apologize for your behavior," Antonio mocked David, "and if I am feeling generous I may only slap you about a bit. It all depends on you," he said with glowing eyes, now almost in a whisper, hardly able to utter the words. His face was an angry mocking mask.

It was a dark and stifling evening. Threatening storm clouds came over the sky about ten o'clock. There was a clap of thunder, and the rain came down like a waterfall. The water fell not in drops, but beat in sheets on cobblestones. There were flashes of lightning every minute and each flash lasted while one could count to three. David felt as though something had fallen on him.

With the odds at five against one, the sly smile on Antonio's face grew broader. Then he spoke slowly to make sure David understood his intentions. "You're not as smart as you think you are, English. I have friends, powerful and dangerous friends, as you see. I know all your filthy games and ugly tricks. We don't like foreigners messing around with our women. Do we, lads?" He looked around as his friends nodded their concurrence with their fists clenched. Antonio continued, "You thought I would not find out about you and Mary? Oh, I know your every move and I know about Sienna. I was coming to your hotel with my friends to see you but as luck would have it, you walked right into my joint. Today I shall take my revenge. You are finished, you hear me?"

David knew that taking down five big guys would be messy and thought of reasoning with him. But here lay the beginning of a chain of events with a shock of terror such as David had never known. David tried again, "You've got it all wrong. I know what you are thinking but if you give me a chance, I can explain about last night."

Antonio's coiled face filled with rage. He dropped his elbow on the table, his chin in his hand, and stared intently at David. For a full minute David scrutinized his face, which he hated with a vengeance. "You do not utter her name with your filthy mouth. As for her, she is going to get it tonight like the wedding night. I bet she told you about that? Tonight will be worse. I am going to give her such a beating, I'll teach her a lesson that she will remember for the rest of her life. But before that, I am going to take care of you."

Listening to him badmouthing Maria, David pointed his index finger in Antonio's face and said, "If you as much as touch, let alone hit, Maria, I swear to God I will hunt you down and kill you. She is finished with you and you'd better leave her alone. And I ought to warn you that all of you put together are no match for my fighting skills. I will take all of you down before you even blink an eye."

The next move from Antonio was something David had fully expected. He leaned back to avoid the swinging punch from Antonio as it swished past only an inch away from his face and then he grabbed Antonio's head in his vice-like grip and smashed it on the table. Quick as lightning, David stood up and grabbed the hair of the two friends and smashed their heads together so hard that there was the sound of mighty clap as if one of the skulls cracked. Both friends fell backwards like timber falling and lay flat on the floor, losing consciousness. The two still standing simply backed off with terror in their eyes.

Antonio, wiping with the back of his hand the blood dripping from his forehead, leaped at David. But David was too fast for him as he ducked to one side and let Antonio fall under his own momentum. Suddenly the big bartender appeared with a large club in his hand, pushing the two still standing friends aside and shouted, "All of you, out of my bar. Take your fight elsewhere. If you insist on continuing then I am calling Carabiniere."

Antonio, with hatred in his eyes, was breathing heavily and using the wall for support as he stood up. "I will be coming back for you," he said, waving his fist at David, "keep looking over your shoulder, for my friends and I will one day cut you up in pieces. You may feel safe for now but it won't last long. I will find you no matter where you go. You're mine." His eyes were blazing and he was spitting as he spoke in anger, trembling with rage and humiliation over losing the fight to David in public. As he was about to leave he said in a low voice so only David could hear him, "Now I'm going to teach that bitch what happens to whores who betray their husbands." Seeing horror in David's eyes, Antonio was now speaking articulately and emphatically, with a smile of triumphant hatred, and again he looked straight into David's stricken eyes and said, "And tomorrow she'll tell you all about it, won't she?"

Without a glance at the bartender and his friends, Antonio rushed from the bar, knocking a couple of chairs out of his way, and headed home. His friends disappeared somewhere in the bar. The bartender gestured with his club at David to leave the bar too. David, realizing the dangerous situation that he had contributed to for Maria, felt that he could never forgive himself if anything were to happen to Maria. He knew regardless what it cost he must stop Antonio. But how does one stop a wounded and hungry predator rushing towards his prey? Force. Brute force. David came out of the bar and was immediately hit with a torrent of rain. He looked around to see if he could catch Antonio and saw him walking hurriedly down the street towards his house. David followed by running after him, all the while shouting his name, commanding him to stop.

Antonio ignored David's shouts and quickened his pace.

35

The stillness of her room put daggers in her mind and Maria sat on her bed with her head resting on her knees, thinking about her life. Why couldn't she follow her heart? Would she, could she ever be free? She raised her head and looked contemplatively at the fresco on her ceiling. *Why do I feel,* she wondered, *that it is me up there? God, why won't you help me, deliver me,* she asked silently. She pressed her balled-up hands against her breasts and reminded herself that she had been faithful to the Lord all her life and now strongly felt His will to grant her the freedom that her soul craved. She got out of bed, slipped her dressing gown on and stood by the window while voices in her head promised her that her time of salvation was approaching fast. She must hold fast to that faith and stay resolute in her commitment to freedom. At an appropriate time her love for David would set her free.

She stood by the window while her mind fed her promises, but something inside her had shattered; something she could only see in pieces, and she failed to conjure its image as a whole. As her heartbeat slowed, allowing her mind to settle, she realized that it was the image of Antonio, her husband, the one she had been true to, that had shattered and at that thought her soul stirred restless because she was left with no option but to drape her dream of freedom over the shattered pieces. She remembered when she gave him her most prized possession, the pendent as a bracelet, in exchange for time she needed to forget what he did to her on the wedding night, and until she could find a renewed interest in him. Twelve years had passed since. Her life as she knew it, unless she found the strength within to take the initiative and leave, from here on would be a veiled sorrow, the reason for it only her heart would know.

She did not want to, but she realized that she did have an option to continue with two separate lives, one within for her sanity and another publicly for her family's happiness. She knew that such a divided life would lead to further sorrow. But in the darkness, she could not see a clear path forward.

Her heart was torn between love and faith. Faith guided her to cherish her husband till death do them part, and love showed her a path of freedom that she had wanted all her life, illuminated with the curious sensation of being loved. In her heart she knew that she was falling from the precipice of faith and that rather than feel guilt and remorse, it made her resolute on her newfound path of love. But an anchor of family honor that was tied to her legs and dropped into the deep waters of traditions, though loosening up, still seemed to be dragging her down.

Now when she had a taste of love, her faith in religious values and obligations was not so much wavering but more behaving like a pendulum. The days when she felt love extended through friendship with David, she began to question the validity or even appropriateness of some of the old-fashioned values of false honor and undue obligation. False and undue, those were the unfair sentiments that haunted her every day she had to look at the face of Antonio. She felt that he was not altogether at fault for he knew nothing different and was only following the rules set out by generations before him, but she was still the victim.

And then there were days when she sat at the dinner table with her grandma, sister and Antonio, and she felt ashamed as if she was caught doing something immoral. She felt like shutting herself away from the world that was luring her to falter. This to her wasn't a fight between good and evil, but merely a desire to find a suitable balance between the old and new. A world full of new joy and life awaited her and she could not help yearning for it. She wondered if she would not have said farewell to David if he had only opened his heart to let her in.

The oscillating pendulum would remind her that she could accept the hand of friendship and love offered by David at the cost of the wrath of society and the anger of her family, or remain oppressed in the false world of religious values and family tradition—the choice was hers. Her struggle between trying to be prudent and yearning for love had a solution and in her soul she knew what it was. She remembered the moment, when going into the hotel, she had inadvertently slipped and David immediately caught her in his strong arms to gently set her back on her feet. Right then, in the confinement of his sturdy arms, she felt an expanse of life, while now she was suffocating in her large house filled with family.

Mary had an ominous feeling of dread for her heart was gradually influencing the tussle in her mind. What she wanted was forbidden. What she was living was unbearable. She felt like a rose whose petals had prematurely started to wither. She realized that the feelings she had for David were more than just an infatuation, and she hesitated to admit even in her silent contemplation that she had found love, true and undeniable. But she knew that they could never be together, the world wouldn't let them. Antonio was jealous of her friendship with David but she also knew that Antonio would kill him if he were ever to find out how she really felt towards David. Those feelings were supposed to be reserved for Antonio; he had been patiently waiting for them. After the wedding night when Antonio had realized the trauma Mary felt from his sexual hunger, he had vowed never to make advances towards her till she invited him back into her bedroom and he had kept his promise, thus far.

She went to the window and sat watching the rain steadily falling from a colorless sky. The grey sky added to the dullness of the day. Heavy clouds, their dark bellies laden with moisture, were slowly drifting into the city as if a giant tarantula was spreading its menacing legs to hold the city in its clutches. As the grey gradually drained the last bit of life out of the day and yielded to the gathering darkness, the moon rose and lit up the sky, but only for a fleeting moment, as dark clouds obliterated it with ease. Somewhere on a distant horizon there was a sudden flash of light and a jagged bolt of lightning like a deadly spear hurled itself towards the earth. A few seconds later the roar of thunder rumbled in her ears. She stood up and waited in anticipation of more thunderous lightning, for she found it exhilarating. The angry clouds did not disappoint her with the power show of lightning and thunder, and it appeared as if the turbulent form was moving closer to the city.

She perched on the edge of her bed and buried her face in the palms of her hands. In the eye of her mind she could see the vague form of her father's face who, whenever she was melancholy, would tell her about the true sense of happy living, saying that hope is latent in every wish and it creates the beginning of a golden web of one's dreams. So why had her hopes led her to a web where she felt trapped? "Oh, Dad, why did you leave me alone like this, and why did you have to go away so young? I wish you were here now for you would have understood me," she murmured quietly. She did not get up from her bed and let the darkness engulf her room.

36

Sudden and frequent lightning filled the room with eerie bright light as if to expose dark secrets. Consumed in the darkness of the night filled with her sighs of despair, she wept silently. She now sat all balled up with her chin resting on her knees, and with downcast eyes stared into the darkness. Suddenly she thought she heard noises. They were muffled and for a moment she thought she might have imagined them. There was no letting up in thunder and lightning and the voices she heard were distinctive even in the roar of continuing thunder, for these voices were close.

With a narrowing of her brows, she stood up and went back to the window to look down on the street below. In the diffused light of the lamppost she saw two figures exchanging blows. Two drunks in the middle of a street fight, she thought. She was about to turn her back on the ugly scene when something stopped her. She looked again and aided by a crack of lightning, she saw what she had dreaded. Her secret was out as David and Antonio were fiercely engaged in a battle right under her window. Their exchange of blows looked fierce but it was like watching a silent movie for the sheets of rain pounding on nearby rooftops had blanketed their cries.

The room palpitated with white light for two seconds, the full-length mirror glared supernaturally. Maria clutched her bible from her bedside table. All was dark again, the thunder clapping directly. There came another slash of lightning.

The night seemed to open and shut. It was a pallid vision of a ghost-world between the clanging shutters of darkness. David and Antonio threw punches at each other spasmodically. In spite of her tumultuous feeling, the thunder impressed her with a sense of fatality. The night opened, revealing the violent scene below, instantly to shut again with blackness. Then the thunder crashed. Mary felt as if some secret were being disclosed too swiftly and violently for her to understand. The thunder exclaimed horror on the matter. She was sure something was happening to her. The rain came down with a rush, persisting with a bruising sound upon the rooftops above and the cobblestones in the street below.

The execution of her friendship with David, staged there before her eyes as if to warn those who dare interfere with the sanctity of her marriage, was unfolding blow by blow. Suddenly a broken beer bottle appeared in Antonio's hand and like a savage animal he charged at David and cut his face with the sharp edge of the glass. Maria screamed from her window asking them to stop, but her scream was extinguished by the burst of thunder. David on his unsteady legs tumbled backward a bit and touched his face with his hand as blood started to pour out from the deep cut. Under the dim light of the lamppost she could make out streaks of red washed by rain, as if the gods of fidelity accepted the sacrifice.

A feeling of intense hate suddenly sprang up in her heart like a sudden bolt of jagged lightning. Its deafening roar she heard in her head and she felt a shock wave pass through her. Her fists clenched, she pounded the windowsill and shouted for them to stop. Dripping with the spray of rain, she leaned out of the window as far as she could and shouted at Antonio to put a stop to this madness.

Antonio heard her voice and looked up and in his face, contorted with hatred, hatred for her, she saw signs of death. He had his arm raised, with the broken bottle, and was about to plunge it again in David's face but momentarily he froze at her shrieks. That was all David needed to regain his balance and in a murderous rage he clenched his right fist and in one mighty blow hit Antonio under his raised chin and sent him crashing to the ground.

And then suddenly, as if the movie had stopped, the fight ceased, but the night was still filled with the constant drone of rain. With his head hanging low David was leaning against the lamppost as if catching his breath as Antonio was lying face down and motionless under the window in the street. David regained his balance, pushed forward away from the lamppost and steadied himself to walk away into the darkness as if walking out of her life, for he did not look up at her.

She repeatedly cried out his name and appealed to him to stop, to stay where he was but rain pounding now harder than ever silenced her screams. As the street below lit up with the blinding brightness of a lightning bolt, he was gone. David, as she imagined, had abandoned her. No, she could not lose him, a scream erupted and suddenly she hated everything in her life, the ancestral house, her family, the city of Florence, and her husband, whose body lay below in the street. Especially Antonio, why could he not understand her and let her go? Fueled by her increasing hatred, a silent fury began to build in her. She had decided to put an end to this miserable life, once and for all. She looked down below and stared at Antonio's body and waited for it to stir. The storm seemed to have intensified and the empty street below was lashed with pounding rain. Mary's heart mirrored the intensity of the storm as she reached her decision. He was not coming back.

A few minutes later she closed the window, something she had never done before, and in that, shut out the life outside her bedroom. She went as if sleep walking to the bed and sat on its edge. Closing her eyes opened a window in her mind through which the events of the past twenty minutes played like a slow motion, black-and-white movie. It was all over, finally, and she let out a deep sigh of surrender.

37

Her marriage was over. Just like that, in the blink of an eye, Antonio was gone. Antonio—husband and oppressor, provider and tormentor, victim and victimizer. No man had ever made her family happier or her more miserable.

It was Affonso who woke up with Maria's phone call informing him of the death of Antonio. He turned up at her house to take her statement and seal the crime scene. Kitty, who came home late after a party, was devastated by the news and wept for Mary. Mary consoled her. First thing in the morning at dawn, Affonso went to David's hotel and found him missing. He questioned the hotel staff and they confirmed that they had not seen him since yesterday evening. His bed was still made and his bathroom tidy. With the hotel owner's permission, Affonso searched David's room but found nothing.

Later that morning a warrant was secured and the authorities at the airport, railway station and bus depot were alerted. Police set up various road checkpoints to ensure David could not escape. Satisfied with the various security measures, Affonso questioned the two burly, slightly bruised friends of the late Antonio and they confirmed the altercation that took place at the bar. In a sworn statement, they confirmed the threat David had uttered regarding killing Antonio. Affonso held a press conference announcing they were treating Antonio's death as murder with a suspect that they had yet to apprehend.

The press in their evening edition as well as the local television news gave sensational coverage of the crime, highlighting the perils of tourism to the local community along with the name and description of David as the prime suspect. They asked the public to assist the authorities in providing any information that may lead to his capture, cautioning not to approach David directly as he was a trained military man who if provoked could be dangerous.

David, lying in a hospital bed with a couple of broken ribs and several stiches on his cheek, was rather bewildered by all this sudden news frenzy on television and buzzed the nurse. He explained that he was the person authorities were seeking but he was innocent of any crime as Antonio was alive when he left the fight last night. Nevertheless, he asked the nurse to contact the police and tell them where he was.

Within minutes Affonso with a few supporting policemen arrived at the hospital and arrested David. Ignoring his condition, they cuffed and dragged him to the police station. The next morning the press hailed their campaign of seeking public support as a success and congratulated Affonso.

Affonso, who never believed David's intention of writing a book, suspected that he was trying to take Kitty away from him. Affonso could not tolerate this, even if his love for Kitty was one-sided. To him this was a wonderful opportunity presented to him as a gift by the hand of providence to eliminate David. Affonso wanted David convicted and quickly went about gathering evidence. He unearthed many incriminating facts to prove the motive—statements from the hotel owner where David and Mary spent the night during the storm, from Lorenzo about their many secretive get-togethers, from friends and the owner of the bar where the fight first started, and finally, from Mary, who witnessed David landing the killer punch.

Affonso also approached the authorities in England and gathered information on David's background, his military training, and combat experience to establish his ability to kill with his bare hands.

Affonso, jealous of David, did not openly display his dislike for David due to his closeness to Kitty, but did intimidate David to confess. Through his police friends he put pressure on David that one way or another they would eventually establish David as responsible for the death of Antonio. The police offered that if David confessed to accidental death and helped police successfully retrieve the missing valuables, then they would go easy on him and make a deal for leniency.

The public prosecutor reviewed all this information and decided that there was enough evidence and motive to initiate criminal proceedings. As the legal threat started to escalate, David realized that he needed help and called his mother, who informed his father. David's father arrived soon after he heard the news and after a brief meeting with David, searched for and appointed the best defense attorney money could buy in Florence. David's father told the police to go to hell, for he believed in David's innocence and was convinced that his initiative in hiring the best legal brains in Florence would lead to David's acquittal.

The defense attorney carefully went over every statement and personally went to talk to all those who gave statements, and found that though the statements were true, they were conveniently not complete. He had particular interest in what Mary had to say for she was the only eyewitness to the fateful fight.

He then looked at the forensic report and questioned the medical examiner who confirmed that the death was likely to have been caused by head trauma from a blunt instrument and not as a result of blows exchanged between David and Antonio. The police report that was very short had details of Antonio's gold watch and bracelet missing and his trouser pockets being turned inside out.

During the preliminary investigation, the defense attorney argued that Antonio's death was due to a severe head trauma caused by a single mighty blow. The forensic examination could not clearly establish the exact nature of the weapon used except it consisted of a hard and rough surface. But there was no evidence of a murder weapon and no witnesses at the time the fatal blow occurred. Since the downpour that night had washed away the dirt where Antonio had fallen there were no footprints. The only eyewitness was Maria and she had given a sworn statement that she clearly saw David hurt and walking away from the fight and Antonio still standing, swearing and cursing at David. Antonio was still alive when David left the scene.

She knew she had not told the complete truth for Antonio was lying perhaps unconscious when David left, and she expected that one day the Lord would punish her for her lies. David was confused that night and had no reason not to believe the statement given by Maria.

The defense attorney along with David's father during one of his visits told David that there was no need to worry. He was confident David would be acquitted of all alleged charges. When David queried the attorney, he replied with a strange grin, "They say that the devil is in the details so when reason fails, the devil helps."

The defense had argued that the expensive and rare pendant bracelet as well as the gold watch missing from Antonio's wrist was the motivation for an opportunist who had hit Antonio on his head to steal his valuables. This argument was supported by the fact that the trouser pockets of Antonio were turned inside out as if someone had searched for a wallet. An extensive search by police failed to produce the gold watch, bracelet, and the wallet.

The defense in its opening argument had reminded the chief prosecutor that all the evidence produced by the police to seek conviction against David was circumstantial and therefore the chief prosecutor must find David not guilty, exonerate him of all charges. He had nothing else than simply an eyewitness account of Mary placing David there, as she said he left before the time of the murder. David's case was further supported by the fact that the missing valuables and the murder weapon were never discovered. Unless these valuables could be found, the defense vigorously argued and reemphasized, there was no case against his client and he asked the public prosecutor to drop all charges.

The chief prosecutor was eventually convinced that the police could not produce compelling evidence to justify conviction against David and dropped all charges against him, allowing him to go free.

David collected his belongings from the jail office and as he turned around he saw both Maria and his father waiting in the sitting area. Maria looked tired as if she had not slept for days. Seeing David, she roused herself, made an effort to smile, and framed a few words of congratulations, but the smile expired, and the sentence was abandoned unfinished. She put on her sunglasses, shut the Bible, and pushed her chair back from the table. And then she alone walked out of the place, leaving David behind with his dad.

David had sometimes read Mary's unspoken thoughts. But now he only wanted her to be happy, especially since she had her freedom.

David knew by her dry eyes that regardless of what she had said in the past, she was resolved to consider him a friend to the last, because to believe him otherwise would give her no pleasure, only a sense of mortification. She had told him sometime back that she considered herself to be an excellent judge of character..

38

Affonso was livid and if he disliked David before, he hated him now. Upon hearing the verdict he had cursed David and remained convinced that he was responsible for Antonio's death. He vowed to find the missing valuables and the murder weapon and to put David back behind bars for the heinous crime he believed he had committed. The truth was that he could not tolerate Kitty being friendly with him and, blinded by jealousy, was determined to eliminate David from her life. Through a friend Affonso delivered a message to David saying that police were convinced of his crime and if he was smart he would leave the country and go back home while he still had the chance.

David's father asked David to accompany him back to England. David wanted to see his mother and reassure her. However, he had not yet accomplished what he had set out to do. He promised his dad that he would soon visit but not immediately. He had a few loose ends to tie up, but it would not be long now before he returned to his mother. Reluctantly, David's father left, for he detested foreign lands.

Kitty was saddened by the sudden and horrific death of Antonio but at the same time felt relieved that David was in clear. She did not want any friends of hers to be wrongfully implicated in their family affairs, even if it was a murder case. She liked David and knew that just like Affonso, Antonio too was jealous of David's friendship with Kitty and Mary. Italian men, she always said, were protective and covetous toward their women. Something that over the time has never changed.

If there was anyone in particular who took Antonio's death to heart, it was Maria. She supported the police inquiry actively but soon after David's acquittal, she shut herself off in her bedroom. She imprisoned herself in the house, which now she hated vehemently. The great, rambling mass of a place seemed evil to her, a menace over her. She was no longer its mistress, she was its victim.

She refused to go out and to even come down for meals. Kitty took her meals to her bedroom that became Maria's prison. Kitty suggested to Maria that they should invite David for supper and maybe his company would bring some cheerfulness into their lives. Maria refused and reminded Kitty that a death in the family required proper mourning and not cheerful company. Days melted into weeks and Maria continued to refuse to face the outside world.

A few weeks elapsed and summer began to relinquish its exuberance to the solemnity of the gradually descending autumn. One day David sat in an outdoor café not far from Maria's house and watched the intensifying colors of the setting sun. Gold was its color; he closed his eyes to gather his thoughts, of his beloved's hair, the hue of the setting sun. In his mind he repeated this line over and over again and each time he felt as if he was physically getting closer to Maria, hoping for reconciliation with his friend in reality and his lover in fantasy. His closed eyes seemed to have conjured up an image of her that his inner self could hold, hug and caress—an experience he'd never had before. David spent many such sunsets in front of Maria's house wondering if she was watching him from her bedroom window, but it remained firmly shut.

David knew that the bigger picture of his new life was made of perhaps a million pieces, but somehow he also knew that Maria was a part of it, an essential part without which his picture of life would make no sense.

Kitty resumed her duty as a guide but now spent only short periods of time with David during which discussions always revolved around Maria. One day and at Kitty's invitation, David came to the house and had tea with her and her grandmother, but Maria refused to come down. After Antonio's death, the grandmother's attitude towards David had softened but she still offered little in the form of conversation. Her overall attitude remained characteristically stern and she asked direct questions such as when David was planning to return to his homeland. She believed in managing life's obstacles by removing them.

David, rather than be dismayed as he was the first time when he was introduced to Grandma, now always found her on the periphery of interesting to amusing. She had a certain aura of her class and time that captivated people. A certain superciliousness of look, coolness of manner, nonchalance of tone, expressing her sentiments on the point of misconception, without committing them to outright rudeness. A scorn that, however, whether covert or open, had now no longer the power over David it once possessed. As he sat between the two ladies, he was surprised to find himself at ease under the total neglect of the one and the attention of the other—Kitty did not charm, nor did grandma disturb him. He felt comfortable, as the saying goes, 'in his own skin.'

Actually David was relieved that no one in the Zuccato family held a grudge against him or in anyway blamed him for the sad death of Antonio, but he was disturbed by the way Maria had been ignoring him. He had wondered if Maria in her mind was not convinced of David's innocence, but then she did tell the truth to the police. Or did she? No, no, he definitely was alive, for David knew he had landed a powerful punch but not hard enough to kill someone. She as the only eyewitness had the potential to sway the chief prosecutor's decision. David was thankful, but could not comprehend this silent treatment. David had always found Maria's silence unsettling and wondered what secrets she held. He wished she would come out and argue if she must, to clear the air between them. He would rather face a just sentence if he were guilty of killing Antonio than this silent ongoing torture.

His visits to the Zuccato family for tea became a regular event but Maria remained confined to her bedroom. But Maria had not objected to him coming to their house. He began to bring flowers for Maria that were sent to her room and the word of thanks was always conveyed back to him, but Maria did not come out of her room to meet with him. Time passed slowly and gradually the summer faded into the arrival of autumn. Autumnal colors turned the city of Florence from an exuberant young girl of summer to a gracious lady of fall.

Book III
Florence, Italy

Autumn 1983
"A love that blossoms in spring bears fruit in autumn."

39

The glory of autumnal foliage owes its brilliance to the kindness of the sun. David wondered if perhaps an initiative was needed from him to bring Maria out of her mourning. Like love, kindness needs to be expressed and not just felt. So on one of his visits to Maria's house, David suggested to Kitty that she allow him to take the tea to Maria's room. Grandma's expression remained passive and Kitty agreed, so David made his way with a tray filled with a few sandwiches and a pot of tea and softly knocked at Maria's bedroom door. David had been preparing a speech to either apologize, for what he did not know, or ask clarification as to why has she been ignoring him. All he wanted to do was to let her know that he cared and the only message he wanted to convey was that since he had been acquitted, his friendship with Maria should remain unblemished. To this end he was prepared to discuss, argue and if necessary, again, apologize.

He knocked at Maria's bedroom door and stood outside listening for some movement inside. A few moments passed and then Maria opened the door. She looked like a wounded person or one who has undergone some terrible physical suffering. Her brows were knitted, her lips compressed, her eyes feverish. She was silent, as deeply hurt as though it were a first wound, forgetting that for twelve years the man she mourned had lost no chance to inflict pain on her. Like a soaring bird struck on the wing by a vulgar shot, she seemed to have sunk into a dull depression.

He had expected her to be sad but not tormented. Was it too early to be interfering like this, he wondered, and felt guilty. All this passed vaguely and fleetingly through his brain, but looking at her more intently, he saw that the suffering creature was so weary that he felt suddenly sorry for her and in a way glad that he'd made the attempt to be with her.

When she began to retreat in terror, it sent a pang to his heart. "I did not expect you," she said hurriedly. She, with a slight and uncertain gesture, invited him in and spoke little, as though performing a duty, and there was restlessness in her movements.

"I'm so sorry, Maria," said David and added, "I shouldn't have come. You need time alone."

He turned to go down the stairs.

Maria watched his broad shoulders as he hesitated at the top of the stairs.

David was remarkably good-looking, he was tall, strikingly well-proportioned, strong and self-reliant—the latter quality was apparent in every gesture, though it did not in the least detract from the grace and gentleness of his movements.

David turned and gave Maria a pleading look. He himself was pale, but it was a healthy pallor, he seemed radiant with freshness and vigor. His face was always more serious and thoughtful than cheerful, but youthful, lighthearted, irresponsible, full of laughter. It was natural enough that a warm, open, simple-hearted, honest lady like Maria, who was not quite at ease, should lose her head immediately. Besides, as chance would have it, perhaps she David was for the first time transfigured by her love to take the chance of coming to the house of the man whom he was accused of killing. This had to be more than just courage, perhaps it was love.

"Please come in and sit down. You come, no doubt, after talking with Kitty and grandma. Allow me—not there. Sit here." She offered a comfortable seat in a small sitting arrangement in a corner of her large bedroom.

As David put the tray down he casually glanced around for he had never been in Maria's bedroom. It was one of the largest and stateliest chambers in the house. A bed supported on massive pillars of mahogany, hung with curtains in front and back of deep red damask, stood out like a temple in the center, the carpet an unusual turmeric color, the table at the foot of the bed covered with a crimson cloth, the walls were a soft fawn color with a blush of pink, the wardrobe, the chairs were of darkly polished old mahogany. Out of these deep-surrounding shades rose high and glared white the piled-up mattresses and pillows of the bed, spread with a snowy Marseilles counterpane. Scarcely less prominent was an ample cushioned easy chair near the head of the bed, also white, with a footstool before it, and looking, he thought, like a pale throne.

In a corner stood a huge full-length, freestanding mirror; his fascinated glance involuntarily explored the depth it revealed. A sitting area comprising an ornate coffee table and two sofa seats, two large bookshelves stocked with books on a variety of subjects and a small mahogany writing desk and chair, and with a high ceiling and large window that was closed, a fern plant on the floor by the window. The room looked uncluttered even with more furniture than necessary. It was meticulously clean, with a colorful fresco on the ceiling and beautifully blended color scheme on the walls, appealing to the eye and soothing to the soul.

Amongst such beautiful surroundings sat Maria in a black dress with a black scarf around her hair. She tried to smile, but there was something helpless and incomplete in her pale smile. She bowed her head and hid her face in her hands.

David looked at the bible on her bed and he pointed at it and then at her attire, asking, "You do this to satisfy your faith?" It was an odd question for he should have been first asking about her welfare but then such old-fashioned values always irritated him and he could not help himself.

"Suffer and expiate my sin by it, that's what I must do."

"You've done nothing wrong and mustn't blame yourself for any of it."

"I sent you away, that was wrong. I know that a misunderstanding has caused a great distance between us and the journey is largely now mine to make."

"Largely?" David said with a slightly mischievous smile on his face to lighten her mood. At the right time, his remarks in the past had lightened her mood.

"Well, entirely." She missed his intent and answered seriously.

"You like to play your game in the shadow of the guillotine? Come on; don't be so serious, it isn't the end of the world."

David now noticed her look of distress and, concerned for her health, deciding perhaps a more formal approach was needed to re-establish their friendship, asked, "Are you okay? You look a little pale."

"I am not pale at all…. No, I am quite well," she snapped almost brusquely and angrily, changing her tone and straightening her spine to peek at the full-length mirror, then added, "just tired."

"I'm sorry, David," she said, leveling her tone, "it has been overwhelming." She seemed willing to mend differences with David now that he had taken the initiative to be here.

David let a few moments of silence soothe her. Maria sat quietly now watching David pour tea and he stole a look at her attentively, deliberately, then he continued pouring the tea. In the past whenever there had been moments that sent Maria into her silent moods, David had felt anxious and frightened. Today again he was frightened at the deep blue blaze of her eyes, and by her stillness, sitting there in her bedroom in her great house. Grandmother and Kitty both had given Maria and David some space, perhaps in the hopes that David's company may bring some reprieve to Maria's troubled heart, as they remained downstairs.

"I've done wrong again. Grandma has always told me that I am unlucky and cannot touch anybody without hurting them. She says I've a destructive force, anyone I embrace I injure."

"And these thoughts weigh on your spirits now, Maria, when we are together? Forget visionary woe, your grandma doesn't know everything, and think only of here and now. You say you care about our friendship, yes—I will never forget that, it is a precious sentiment for me and I feel you too cherish such a feeling, you cannot deny it. When you utter beautiful words about us, trust me, those words do not die inarticulate on your lips. I hear them, thoughts too complex for some to understand perhaps, but sweet as music. I think it is a glorious thing to have the hope of spending time in your company, Maria, because I care for you. Do you hear me? The question is do you care for me, Maria? Do you really? Say it if you do."

Although Maria had been silent moments before, she had never been so utterly still. She looked thin and fragile. "Are you going to shut yourself off from the world like this forever?"

"I alone know how to mourn for him as he deserves."

As they sipped on hot tea in silence, David had an idea. "Would you," he asked in an amicable tone, "like me to read something to you? I noticed you have some fascinating books on your bookshelves." She seemed to like the idea of listening to his voice without having to think of what to talk about under such awkward circumstances, and nodded.

He got up and, after a few minutes of browsing, pulled out a copy of *Leaves of Grass* by Walt Whitman, then walked back with it to his chair. As he sat, he tapped the book cover and said, "This book is remarkable for its delight in and praise of the senses during a time when such candid displays were considered immoral. I am talking about the mid-nineteenth century when Whitman first published this. Prior to this, most English poetry relied on symbolism, allegory, and on the religious and spiritual aspects but he in this book exalted the body and the material world in an amazing and unparalleled way. This is one of my favorite books and in it I have always found answers to difficult questions."

"Thank you. I appreciate your coming up here and not giving up on me."

David smiled, delighted to be with her again. She fascinated David, as if some perfume about her intoxicated him. So he went on helplessly with his reading.

The deep, soothing sound of David's voice was like the whispering wind flowing through a lush garden on a warm summer day. Mary watched David's lips move as he read.

She felt guilty at times like this, thinking about David, for only a few weeks had passed since Antonio had passed away, but she did not resist such feelings of love as they continued to soothe her soul. Watching his soft lips, she felt him in her soul and in all her veins. His love was in her veins, but it was not an appropriate time to evoke it. She was like a forest, like the dark interlacing of the twisted and turned oak trees, humming inaudibly with myriad unfolding buds. Meanwhile the birds of desire were mute but not quite asleep in the vast interlaced intricacy of her body. She watched him with wide, vague, veiled eyes. *Yes, I'm sure he will be mine,* she thought as she slowly closed her eyes, as if to hold his spirit within her.

With a promise to meet tomorrow for a morning walk by the Arno River, he took the tray, bid her farewell and went quietly out of the room. His ideas were all tangled. He went dreamily through the drawing room, putting the tray on the table and then out of the house.

She was back in his life. He walked down the street whistling a tune he loved without caring about what the exact words were.

40

At dawn the darkness retreated, yielding to the growing murmur of life springing up with the morning. Strings of sunlight scaled the window and the morning glow and its gentle warmth woke her to a new day. She felt good as if the gods had made her new promises.

There was a curious sensation in her heart that started to germinate like a seedling does when exposed to warm sun and water. She felt like reopening the window that had been shut since the day Antonio died. She went towards the window as if walking in her sleep and stopped, holding the window handles. Outside there was a bright sunny day rapidly growing out of the dawn light and sunrays were streaming through the windowpane that lit up her face. She closed her eyes and saw drifting red suns under her amber lids. The elated feeling in her heart was growing, as if the brilliant glow from every windowpane of her large window could lead her home—a veritable lighthouse on the white-capped sea.

Her hands moved involuntarily and a fresh warm breeze bathed her face with renewed energy. She opened her eyes and placed the lone fern plant back on the windowsill, still thriving in its heavy blue pot, welcoming her back. She gently touched the leaves, excited to let life come back into her room, as the window curtains billowed in the gentle breeze.

When she arrived, David was waiting for her by the riverbank. The mist hung over the waters, over the wide shallows of the river, and the sun, coming through the morning, made lovely purple-orange lights beneath the bluish haze, so that it seemed like the beginning of the universe. And there was a Peregrine falcon hovering above, riding the thermals, seeming to have spotted a Zitting Cisticola that was noisily proclaiming its presence with its eponymous call around a weedy area by the side of the river. Ever rising higher and higher, the falcon continued to circle above his prey, like some strange symbol in the sky. David and Maria watched in amazement.

How lovely the little river is, she marveled, with its silvery ever-changing wavelets. It seemed to her like a living companion while they wandered along the bank and listened to its low, equable voice, like someone humming a melodious tune. She always loved the bridge of Ponte Vecchio.

She looked over to see David walking along by her with his head down in deep thought. The sun tinged the water with a faint hue of soft pink under the transient glance of this autumnal sun. As the sun rose higher, it cast its golden tones mingled with amber upon the casements of the chateau; the effect was that of a painted picture.

"So you pray a great deal, Maria?" he asked, breaking her reverie. Maria did not speak. He stood beside her waiting for an answer. "What would I be without God?" she whispered, glancing at him with suddenly moist eyes, clutching tighter her little purse. "And what does God do for you?" he asked, probing further. Maria was silent a long while, as though she could not answer. Her chest heaved with emotion. *Be silent. Don't ask. You don't really want to know,* this and several other interrelated thoughts raced through her mind.

"He does everything," she whispered finally, looking down again.

She stole a glance at him with incredulous wonder, thinking, *What is it that he wants to know?*

They now had been walking by the River Arno for over twenty minutes in the soft morning light but were unable to find a suitable conversation to ease the tension between them. "Tell me," he asked suddenly, looking almost cheekily at her as if taking pleasure in his own light-hearted approach, "the house," David paused as if wondering should he or should he not voice his thoughts and then deciding in favor of the former, continued, "your house, why is it so important to your family that they would sacrifice the happiness of their own child for keeping it?"

And as he said this David screwed up his eyes and winked, a good-humored, crafty look passing over his face. The wrinkles on his forehead were smoothed out, his eyes contracted, his features broadened and he suddenly had a nervous laugh, looking away from Maria as if trying to de-emphasize the importance of his question.

Maria considered this question that seemed to lead somewhere in a roundabout way. "I felt that you were eventually going to ask a question like that," she said, glancing at him. "I dare say you did. But how is it to be answered? You seem committed to drag it out of me, aren't you?" Mary answered in a lighthearted tone too, but then her mood turned serious and in a contemplative voice she explained, "Unlike my mother, I'm not obsessed, but in a strange way I do love this house. Look at its structure, it's as if each year of its existence has slowly chipped away at the optimistic belief that everything will turn out all right in the end, that happily ever after is the bookend to every story. Yet in its bowels are stories of sorrow and agony. I realize, as I stand surrounded by its four walls, that I will never have the fairy-tale ending. But just like the weary buildings with a lifetime of living etched in their aging walls offering their own sweet perspective, my life will in the end have its own bittersweet story. And isn't that what our lives are, stories?"

David was surprised at this for he had thought that she would be angered rather than saddened by his question, for she was the victim of her house and opening the old wound may stir strong feelings in her.

"No, not at all. If you prefer not to talk about it then let us just forget that I ever asked about the house. Let us talk about something else."

"You are a bit touchy this morning," she smiled and then suddenly became quite serious, like a dark cloud compromising the brilliance of the sun, as she asked, "you seem to have picked up quite a bit of the history of our country. Tell me, have you studied the architecture of our old buildings?"

"Not much, I am afraid," David admitted. He had been hoping to learn about the fascinating architecture of the old buildings that surround the major cities of Italy. David believed that like the paintings of masters, the Italian buildings hid their mysterious stories in their intricate architecture.

"Then allow me," Mary said in a soft voice, "I know it looks like any other old house in Florence. But the history of our house is what sets it apart from others and has the effect of some voluminous phrase, say, even a musical that dropped first into words and notes without sense and then, when finished, turns into a fine symphony. You see, some local historians believe that our house belongs to the fifteenth century because one of its outside walls bears a carved statue of Madonna. The painting and carving of religious portraits on the outside walls of homes, especially those of stucco, was customary during the fifteenth century, as indeed it is today in many Italian cities. For hundreds of years people have claimed to witness some of these statues weeping blood as tears. The Madonna on the outside wall of our house is one of such statues, making this house worthy as a place of worship. We live in a blessed house of Madonna."

"Weeping Madonna," said David, keeping his tone gentle, careful of Maria's feelings, "do you believe in it? I mean, with all the problems you and your family have been exposed to, how does that make sense in a blessed house worthy of worship?"

"It is because the Virgin Mary has not shed tears for centuries for the salvation of the people of our house. Don't ask me how but in my heart I feel that she soon will."

David kept quiet and simply looked at her, not as much in disbelief but more so with sympathy.

"You don't believe me? Let me tell you a little more about it. Such religious decorations found their mark in history due to a curious event that took place two years after the October 4, 1483 feast day of St. Francis of Assisi. On October 4, 1483, the house of Diotallevi d'Antonio Santilli on the road between Spopeto and Trevi was painted on the outside wall with a portrait of the Madonna. A passerby noticed the Madonna shedding tears of blood and then neighbors flocked to the scene and as the news spread, the people from nearby towns came to see the prodigious occurrence.

"A notary of Trevi was alerted and he, too, rushed to the scene. He described the prodigy in writing and recounted many miracles performed by the crying Madonna that he witnessed. On August 21, 1485, one week after the start of the miracle, the first Holy Mass was offered in a small chapel that was hastily erected by the wall of the Madonna for it was considered that Her tears represented the sympathy of the Madonna for the pestilence which for years had tormented the territory around the city of Trevi. Many religious authorities believed that the Virgin's blood-tears were shed for the ills and faithlessness of contemporary society to stimulate prayer and devotion.

"People were overwhelmed by this miracle and raised money and on March 27, 1487, work was begun to construct a new church for the Mother of God. Such was and is the power of Madonna to bind society and families together through faith and prayers."

David was delighted to see Maria talking passionately about her convictions, distracting her from the recent tragedy. He wanted to encourage her to continue, so asked, "And you believe that one day someone in this house will have the power of prayers to evoke Madonna? To release your family from long sufferings and finally bring back the opulence that once your family possessed?"

"Not someone...." She let her sentence trail off. David clearly understood the implication and felt concern for he never believed in such far-fetched stories. He stopped to face her and held both her hands and gazed into her blue eyes. He gently squeezed her hands and said, "I don't mean to offend anyone, but I have a different perspective on religion. A visionary man invented religion, and the figurehead of religion that is God. The purpose for this was actually quite virtuous, simply to give people hope. Hope to those who were facing hopeless situations. And it is this, I firmly believe, that has saved humanity from many dark times in our history. But the fanatics turned it to their advantage by using it as a weapon against those who are loving, caring, forgiving, and above all hopeful, to exploit them. Centuries have passed and will pass, and the ignorance will continue to thrive in so-called civilized society, if blind faith is allowed to continue in the name of religion."

Maria's eyes expressed surprise, as if searching for the true intent of his suggestion. Slowly a smile appeared that gradually stretched to a full grin and then suddenly she broke out in an uncharacteristic peal of laughter. When she finally caught her breath, she said, "You had me there for a moment." She shook her head as her laughing fit settled and, gently releasing her hands from his and punching him on his arm, said, "You are so funny, David."

"I'm dead serious," is what David wanted to say but instead he kept quiet. He often wondered how and why an intelligent mind such as that of Maria's, which was quite capable of fighting any adversity in the path of progress and building fortune from nothing, would be so dependent upon and obsessed with religious intervention. But for now he was happy to see her laugh.

He had succeeded in breaking her mourning spell.

41

"There is no one—no one in the whole world now so unhappy as I am," she cried softly, seeming not to hear what he said about the red dress she wore after wearing black for such a long time. They were out for dinner in an expensive restaurant that David chose the very next day after their walk by Arno River, and she suddenly broke into quiet weeping. A feeling not unfamiliar to him flooded his heart. He did not struggle against it. Two tears hung on his eyelashes. "Oh Maria," he said furtively, drying his eyes with the corner of his crisp white napkin, "I wish I could make you happy."

"Then do something for me?" she said suddenly with a faint smile on her face as she viewed him with moist eyes, this tough, army-trained fighter shedding tears for her sadness.

"Anything," he smiled back, closing his eyes to drive his tears away.

"Let me into your life. Tell me more, anything about you and your family. I would like to think we are still friends. I feel guilty of once saying goodbye to you and would like to be assured that you have forgiven me."

"Forgiven you?" David smiled broadly now. "You have done nothing wrong to be asking for forgiveness. You are a lady of amazing values and I respect you for that. Okay, if you really want to know, then it all started like I told you. My father used to say to me that every soldier on the battlefield has a singular duty—to kill or be killed. If you kill then you have done your duty in the name of protecting your nation. If you are killed then you are a hero. The killing is merely a condition of victory, but the victory itself lies in the feat achieved. Do you know what he said at the airport when I was being sent to the front to fight the Falkland war?" David smiled as his dad's words rang in his ears as they often did when he thought of the Falklands. "Son, with a gun in your hands, instinct in your gut, and blood on your boots, you're about to learn about soldiering. This is what you have been trained for. Be a good soldier and make me proud."

"How old were you when you went there as a soldier?" Maria asked almost with the inquisitiveness of a child listening to a story.

"Um, I was twenty-two. And as regards soldiering, well, I didn't learn much about soldiering but did discover a thing or two about myself. Killing in the name of freedom and peace is still killing. The appeal in the eyes of a dying soldier, enemy or not, for mercy uttered in his dying breath with a bullet in his head is beyond any cause for killing in the name of religion or patriotism. And God have mercy on your soul if you are the soldier who put the bullet in his head, for those eyes will haunt you and gnaw at your soul till your dying days."

Mary asked, "David, you don't have to tell me if you don't want to, but I feel that there is more to it than what you are telling me. Did you kill people in this war? Is this why you always look so sad when you talk about your father and the Falklands?"

A momentary hesitation aided him in gathering his thoughts. He clasped his hands and placed them on the table as he leaned forward and whispered, "I did worse than killing." He looked deep into her eyes and uttered, "What is in you that wants me to bare my soul?"

The images of the war played like a movie in his head. Some, of friendship and camaraderie, he liked and tried to clutch at, but they faded and all the while there was an oppression within him. He shivered once and the slight tremble still persisted, but that too was giving fuel to this unpleasant sensation.

"David," she whispered. "David, are you okay?"

"Maybe I should tell you what happened out there," he said in a contemplative voice. "I had a younger brother; he was only twenty when we both together went to war. I was trained in SAS and he preferred infantry. On the 28th of May, 1982, he was commanding the Second Battalion of the Parachute Regiment on operations on the Falkland Islands. They had orders to attack enemy positions around the settlements of Darwin and Goose Green. He found the enemy well dug in, the Battalion was held up just South of Darwin by a well-prepared and resilient enemy on an important ridge. Our intelligence turned out to be incomplete and a number of casualties were received. My brother radioed in and asked to abort the mission and airlift his troops. The authorities turned him down and asked him to hold the position and stay on offensive."

"That is ridiculous, it is like condemning him to death!" cried Maria. "I thought the military looked after their own?"

"In a war they call it collateral damage," said David in a bitter tone and then continued. "In order to better read the battle and to maintain the momentum of his attack, my brother took forward his reconnaissance party to a higher ground. Despite persistent, heavy and accurate fire the reconnaissance party gained the higher ground, almost the same height as the enemy position. From here he directed mortar fire, in an effort to neutralize the enemy. However, the enemy continued to pour effective fire onto the Battalion advance, which under increasingly heavy artillery fire was in danger of faltering."

Maria gestured for the approaching waiter with menus to hold back. The waiter turned away to give the couple more time.

David, oblivious to his surroundings, felt as if he was in a trance and in an unwavering tone continued, "In his effort to gain a good viewpoint, he was now at the very front of his Battalion. It was clear to him that desperate measures were needed in order to overcome the enemy position, and to save the lives of his troops. It was time for personal leadership and action and he was known for it amongst his peers. He immediately seized a sub-machine gun, and, calling on those around him and with total disregard for his own safety, charged the nearest enemy position. This action exposed him to fire. As he charged up a short slope at the enemy position he was seen to fall and roll backward downhill. He immediately picked himself up and again charged the enemy, constantly firing his sub-machine gun and seemingly oblivious to the intense fire directed at him. He was hit by enemy fire, and fell dying only a few feet from the enemy he had assaulted. Inspired by his heroism, his troops with guns blazing attacked the enemy, who baffled by this blatant act quickly surrendered. The display of courage by my brother had completely undermined their will to fight further."

"David," she said, caressing his arm, "that is enough, the rest can wait."

"You might as well hear the rest of it, too," he said, pursing his lips. Without waiting for her response, he added, "His heroic act set the tone for the subsequent land victory on the Falklands. The British achieved such a moral superiority over the enemy in this first battle that, despite the advantages of numbers and selection of battleground, the Argentinian troops never thereafter doubted either the superior fighting qualities of the British troops, or their own inevitable defeat. This was an action of the utmost gallantry and dashing leadership and courage and for this he was given the Victoria Cross, posthumously, of course."

"Oh, David," she said, quietly sobbing. "I am so sorry about your brother, but why do you blame yourself for it? You should be proud of him."

David paused and then, gazing straight into her big blue eyes, he said, "You don't want to know any more. Trust me, you don't Maria. I've already told you more than I have ever told anyone before."

"Let me in," Maria cried, "let me in on it, please. Tell me what happened."

"I am the one who as a part of an SAS mission sneaked earlier into the enemy territory to gather intelligence. I was double-crossed and deliberately fed wrong information. It is my incompetency that caused my brother his life. I can't help feeling that I wrote his death warrant and am responsible for his death. When he asked for help from the authorities to abort and retreat, I volunteered to fly back in and help airlift the troops, including my brother. But I was denied on the grounds that the situation had turned too dangerous and would result in nothing but unnecessary loss of state property."

"What state property?" she asked.

"Aircraft."

42

Kitty missed Antonio and the unconditional support that he had provided to keep the house and meet all family needs. With him around there were no financial worries for he took care of everyone. He was like a father figure to her and having a male around was a comfort and reassurance. That was all but gone now. Oh, he left a trust to provide for their financial needs, but it was not sufficient to maintain the same luxurious lifestyle as they had when he was alive. Besides, Antonio's family, the owner of all his businesses, was threatening to contest his will as they were not happy with Antonio leaving so much money in the trust for the Zuccato family. Lifestyle adjustments would have to be made and Kitty knew she would have to work harder in finding more money. Maria, too. She would also have to find work. Kitty missed Antonio.

Although she never made it known publicly, every time Kitty was disturbed by tougher times ahead she could not help but put some of the blame on Maria. Why could she not work out her differences with Antonio and be a traditional wife, the one Antonio wanted. She often wondered if David was the root cause of what deepened the gulf between Maria and Antonio. No sooner would she have such thoughts than she would chastise herself, for she knew that she had encouraged David to be Maria's friend and as a good friend does, he had brought some happiness into Maria's world.

But the uncertain future continued to haunt her and she resented Maria's going out with David for walks and dinners. It was too early and the community would not approve of it. She wondered if she could find a way to talk to Maria about it without upsetting her. Although Kitty was a direct person and never shy in expressing her opinion, dealing with a grieving widow was a delicate matter and called for prudence.

Sitting at home doing some paperwork and contemplating such thoughts, Kitty heard footsteps on the landing and saw Maria coming down in a body-hugging black velvet dress and matching black shoes, obviously on her way out to see David. She felt a strange loathing in her heart. How could she? But she remained quiet and Maria, without a glance in her direction, swiftly left the house.

Twenty minutes later and as pre-arranged, Maria met up with David at a café of David's choice. Her blue eyes against the backdrop of her black velvet dress were like two sapphires in a crushed black velvet-lined box and her golden hair danced on her shoulders in a mild breeze. Suddenly David saw Mary's eyes welling up and two tiny tears clung to her eyelashes.

"Why are you crying, do I make you sad?"

"No, you make me happy."

"Then why the tears?"

"I was thinking," she answered, wiping the tears away with a handkerchief she took from her purse, "that my life up until now has been imprisoned by safety and I've my mother and father to thank for it. What a waste it has been, isn't that a sad state of affairs?"

"You know what," David replied as he leaned back in his chair, "you always remind me that I talk too much about my father, but I hardly know anything about yours. Tell me about your father, what was he like?"

"My father died a day after he was involved in a car crash, damn the Italian drivers," she said in a contemplative voice. "On his death bed he was not angry or sad, he repeatedly said to me that God had finally forgiven and delivered him from his burden of wrongdoings done due to his weak character. He never could get along with my mother. Antonio was fourteen years older than me, almost twice my age at the time of our wedding. All these years I have been so distraught and blamed my parents for selling me off in a marriage for money. I believe Dad never forgave himself for what he did and I think that he could not live with the guilt. Oh, in all reality, something died in him on my wedding day, for he never looked happy after that. My dad was so overwrought with grief that on his deathbed he kept apologizing to me for marrying me off to Antonio. Dying men's confessions speak more damning truth than what comes from a babe's mouth."

"I'm sorry that he had to go through such suffering and that you became victim of his mistakes. I was told that his gambling had caused most of the problems. Kitty told me this sometime back."

"Kitty is right, but if my mother had been a better companion to my dad and not been so besotted with the damn house, then maybe, just maybe Dad would have recovered from his obsessions."

"Don't take this the wrong way," David said carefully as he moved to the edge of his chair, holding one of her hands in both of his, "but it seems that your prayers have been answered. Haven't they? You are a free woman now. You can be anything you want to be, right?"

Mary tilted her head as if hesitant to say what she wanted and then haltingly began, "I admit that I sought liberty from Antonio, from our miserable marriage, to find new opportunities, but I never sought opportunities to find liberty. That would have been wrong. You understand what I mean?"

David did not answer the question. Their talk was disrupted by a waiter bringing their order of two glasses of Chianti and 'Spaghetti dell'ubricecone,' for which this little place at Via de Benci was popular amongst Florentines. After the waiter left and they said 'salute,' clinking their wine glasses, Maria resumed speaking. "I don't want to talk about Antonio when we are together. But once and for all, I would like to explain that as cruel as it may seem, he got everything he deserved. That makes me sound harsh but then don't forget that I was his victim. He never understood that physically oriented sexual hunger should be constrained by the boundary of morality for a good reason; that if it is not driven by love, then it is a sickness and must not go unpunished. I will forgive him, but I cannot forget the wrong. Do you believe me, David?"

Her eyes were moist as she asked the question, the question for which she did not wait for an answer and added, "Such a punishment is not provided for in our laws for in the name of traditional rights it seems that man has written his freedom to act like an animal if he wishes. But there is a court of higher laws, His court and He in His own ways sooner or later carries out justice and delivers its victims. I knew all along that one day my faith would deliver me, and that still is my hope, David. In your friendship I see a promise of that hope, am I asking too much of us? I would hate to burden you with my problems by giving our mutual feeling of happiness a label of deeper relationship than what we have now, just being friends. But these are my reasons why I cannot commit more than I already have. I hope you don't mind my being so candid?"

Suddenly two small, white butterflies fluttered up and down in agitated little leaps around her. Instinctively Maria put her hand forward to touch them. David watched her innocent play as they both clinked their glasses again and wished, 'Bon Appetit.'

David would take this relationship at any level she would allow, and reveled in this moment of happiness with her, perhaps as fleeting as the butterflies.

43

The soul is something inside, wrapped in inner truth. She did not care if the world did not understand or care for her quest of inner truth. Day by day and with the help of David, she was rebuilding her life. Waiting any longer in mourning to her was a waste of her life, bestowed upon her as a gift from the Lord. It was her duty, her mission to appreciate that gift by living her life to the full. But should she attain the fulfillment of her life with or without David, was the question.

David on the other hand although a complete gentleman and never imposing had not made secret his wishes and desires. He found it encouraging that Maria was no longer bound by the vows she had taken at her ill-fated marriage and had become quite vocal about her freedom.

The burning colors of autumn were reaching their peak as the season entered into its last phase, turning the city to a festive mood. Various theaters and dances were being performed in the city to celebrate autumn. One beautiful Sunday morning after Maria went to mass David invited her to an early lunch. As they sat in a café by the river enjoying fine wine, David asked, "Do you still feel that you are bound by your faith to mourn your loss in isolation? You shut yourself up for quite a few days after Antonio's death. I was so worried about you. I only ask because I am not one who is guided by faith and find it hard to ask Him to take care of everything."

David did not know what came over him to ask such a question, especially when it was Sunday. She had just come from church, and he was conscious of her terrible inner turmoil.

"The good book says he who searches for knowledge finds sorrows. Are you sure you want to venture out to find knowledge?"

All he wanted was their friendship to grow, and almost expected a rebuff for this hardly well-timed question, but, on the contrary, waking from her silent abstraction, she had offered him an encouraging answer. He felt relieved. David added, "Sure, I want to know where we are heading. Oh, I missed us. We were good together, and we're good together now; our intentions are clear. If people cannot understand our relationship then let us not make their problem ours. Well, to resume," he raised his glass as a tribute to her fighting spirit.

"I think I can understand where you are coming from," she finally spoke. "You may not believe in God, but trust me when I tell you that you have faith. I hate to mention him but men like Antonio have no insight into true faith, the very foundation of which is love. It is not the religion of church that provides guiding light; it is the spirituality of the soul that awakens when you find love. But a man like Antonio in the name of religious faith will continue to persecute women. Yes, he will do that until his faith fails one day and then he will be on the run, most of all from himself. But a woman can't do that, because women are about nothing but the spirituality that is based on truth for truth is love. You can't run away from that. It may be a sad thing for many women are suffering because of their beliefs but it is so. It is just so. And they cannot do anything but to have faith and believe in God."

"Oh, God left this place a long time ago for the reasons that surround us." David liked such debates, provided they were not offensive, and he admired Maria in her willingness to openly discuss her faith so he continued. "There is no point blaming or seeking salvation from Him. He is no longer interested in redeeming humanity for it has crossed that hidden boundary beyond which there is no return. I have seen an example of it in the Falklands. He may have to start all over again. We are on our own and need to create our own salvation. Over two thousand years of teaching and lessons learned should be enough to save a soul or two, don't you agree?"

"Do not slander life," she said to him. "You are ignorant of true love; such love gives happiness that shines in heaven."

They fell silent as they ate their lunch, like a meadow is at midday in summer. The still foliage by the riverside lay sharply defined by the blue of the sky, dragon-flies were flitting among the reeds and the trees along the banks of river. A few couples walked hand in hand along the river shore, the ruddy earth of the path alongside the river glowed, children rushed up and down its banks. What a show of the sparkling river and rich-green landscape while they enjoyed what had become a comfortable relationship.

After the waiter removed the empty dishes he served them espresso. David could sense that several thoughts were whirling in Maria's mind and there seemed to be something she was aching to ask. He wanted to be like an open book, no secrets, no hidden agendas. But before he could say something Maria, putting her espresso cup down, gently said, "David, I know what you are hoping for and somehow I think you feel that the untimely death of Antonio has a hand of providence in it." She paused, and then added, with an assumed indifference, but a marked and significant tone, "You are young, David, and I should say a bit impulsive; perhaps you are not aware of the fact that I'm six years older than you?" She lowered her eyes as if guilty of a crime.

David held his espresso cup pressed against his lower lip, allowing Maria to say more. She again raised her eyes to David, and seemed to examine him warily, then she answered, "You're persistent, I'll give you that. Perhaps foolish, too."

David put his cup down and pushed the saucer with its empty cup away. "I'm going to say something that I've been trying to say to you for weeks, months. Never before have I had the opportunity, but I guess this moment is as good as any." He said this as if speaking to a vision, invisible to any eye but his own. David continued, "Ever since I saw you for the very first time, I have dreamt of our life together, sometimes knowingly and often unknowingly, and today is the first day that my dream has a chance, for you're free, we're free. Together we can have a great life. We can go away, if that suits you, and start our new life somewhere else, anywhere we could be together."

"Sweet David," she said and stretched out both hands for him to hold, which he did with a smile, "what would you have me do? I so dearly want you as a friend, no, actually more than a friend, a soul mate."

"Meet me tomorrow evening," said David excitedly, "there is a dance in a small piazza I know. Let's go there and celebrate our renewed friendship. I will come to your house and pick you up, say, at seven, okay?"

"Tell me where the piazza is and I will meet you there at seven," she responded with a smile.

"That would not be considered proper," he countered then whispered, "I shall come and escort you to our first dance."

Maria realized that David loved her passionately, and yet somehow he had made it impossible for her to embrace the love she felt for him. David held the keys to her happiness, but those keys had unlocked the gates of hell. He had been a mercurial man—passionate, dedicated, jealous, but also loving, generous, and capable of largesse. Perhaps it had been her fault that she had never learned how to handle this man, how to steer through the choppy waters he left in his wake. Could Kitty—more impulsive, more outgoing—have done it differently?

She shook her head as if to throw out such thoughts and drift away into the promise of tomorrow's life.

44

The next evening David arrived at seven and knocked at the door to present a large bouquet of lilies to Maria. She smelled the flowers and closed her eyes as if in ecstasy. "Come on in and sit down. And thank you, these are beautiful."

"So are you." He entered the house behind her and they sat in the drawing room. He looked at her in a quizzical fashion and she noticed it, asking, "What? Why are you staring?"

He cupped his hand around the back of his neck and rubbed it as if he was tense. "Does your family, your grandmother and your sister, want you to wear black for the rest of your life? We are going to a dance, you know."

"This is what's expected of me. It shows respect for the dead and is customary."

"Respect?" His face contorted. "For someone who tormented you all his life?" He let out a sigh of exasperation and, looking straight in her blue eyes, said, "You're you and not what others want you to be. You didn't come into this world with any attachments and one day we will all leave taking nothing with us, so why do these people think they have any right to control your life?"

There was a slight rustling noise in the room as if someone was there. Kitty had silently entered the room, and was listening in to their conversation.

Kitty stood in front of David and stared at him with unyielding eyes. Then she shouted, "I've been watching you two for days, and what you are doing is shameful. I will not let you defile the memory of my brother-in-law. Get out! You're an antichrist. If you had not fought with Antonio then none of this would have happened. I should have never allowed you to get involved with us. Leave my sister alone, leave all of us alone and leave. Out of my house!"

Silence fell as if all the air had been sucked out of the room. David had known for a while that she was upset but was not prepared for such an outburst. He thought that maybe he ought to say something to calm her for she may later regret her blunt remarks. All this time she had been such a good-humored person and suddenly as if the bite of a cobra had poisoned her body and mind, she was spitting fire.

"Kitty, you are making too much of it." David stood up and approached her. "Maria has suffered enough already and her God has given her a chance now to live a normal life. You yourself told me what a miserable time she'd had so why do you want her to continue with this stupid custom of wearing black for so long. She deserves a happy life, don't you agree?"

"You are a despicable man," she said in an acid tone laced with uncontrollable anger, "you are calling us stupid now? You used me to get to Mary and you planted the seeds of doubt in her mind. Every marriage has its ups and downs and Mary and Antonio were managing. He may be gone but I will not let you mess around with Mary while his memories are still alive in this house, in our hearts. Leave us and don't come back or do you want my friend Affonso to drag you out of here? He has not forgotten you, you know?" She clenched her fists, her expression, searing.

The room stood still for an immeasurable second. The silence continued, but somehow the room seemed to flicker and tremble with tacit tension. It was as if each one of its inhabitants knew that a moment of reckoning was at hand, that this was the test they had to meet together or forever be expelled into their own isolated, silent worlds. Together they formed the three points of a triangle, and the least movement on any of their parts would destroy this delicate yet troubled balance.

A cold fury fell over Mary like a steady rain. A twitch, which began in the corner of her eyes and moved slowly down to her lips, showed that her time had come to stand up for her freedom. A few moments ago she did not know how to stop Kitty's barrage but her answer was ready now. She stood and faced Kitty. "I don't quite see,' she answered on behalf of David, "where in particular it states that you are my guardian. I'm not harboring, I assure you, the least disposition to 'throw' myself at anyone. I feel that for the present I've been quite sufficiently thrown about by my family. You cannot tell me what to do."

"Mary, please listen," Kitty urged.

"No, you listen," Mary returned, "would you like me to shut myself in my room for the sake of the neighbors while you go out and party all night? You would like that, wouldn't you?

"If I should feel like going out, am I bound to give you notice, so that you might make appropriate arrangements? Is that your idea?" Mary asked. Then as her sister still stood in silence, "I know that living with him was impossible and now you want to make my living without him equally difficult? Antonio and I were nothing but two people in an extraordinary relationship who unknowingly smothered each other. Hard to admit, but perhaps it is the story of most married couples. Now it is over and I owe my life to no one, especially not to my baby sister. So, back off and let me spend time with my friends the way I want to."

Kitty fixed her with beseeching eyes. "What in the world is the matter with you?" she pleaded. "You don't know what you are saying." Kitty tried to hold Mary's hands but she pulled away. "David has seduced you for his own needs, he is like that. I know such men. They are not good for you. You will be terribly hurt. I will not let David hurt you. Listen to me. Don't go out with him tonight. Please, don't."

But it was oddly, the very next moment, as if she had perhaps been a shade too dramatic, as Mary turned around and in a firm voice that warranted no objections, said to David, "Wait right here." And then she gracefully climbed the stairs back to her room while Kitty and David remained behind in an awkward silence.

There was a difference in the air—even if none other than the supposedly usual difference in truth between man and woman, and it was almost as if the sense of this provoked Kitty. She seemed to be mulling something over in her mind to say or do to stop this shameful act. She appeared to take up rather more seriously than she needed the initiative set by Mary concerning her freedom. Yet she did this too in a way of her own. "Men are too stupid, even you. You didn't understand just now why I tried to stop Mary. But mark my words; I will not let her be hurt by the likes of you. You foreigners are all alike, you come here to cry your sorry stories of back home to get innocent Italian girls to feel sorry for you and sleep with you, and before anyone knows anything you are gone, back to your families. This will not happen to Mary, I promise you. I'll stop you, one way or another, I will stop you." She said the words in a tone so bitter, so hollow, that they stifled the remonstrance of David's pleading.

A few moments passed and David did not respond to Kitty's rhetoric for he did not want the argument to escalate. Suddenly Mary appeared at the top of the stairs and slowly step-by-step descended to where David and Kitty were standing. She was clad in a low-cut, skin-tight, bright red, revealing satin dress that clung to her body like a vine wrapping itself around a tree. She wore a matching pair of shoes and had an air of confidence about her and a firm determination in her gait.

Kitty said nothing but her eyes entreated her; she had moved close to her, half-enclosed her with urgent arms. "Don't do this," she tried to say but choked with emotion, she could not.

"Let's go, David, I'm ready for that dance." And then as Mary brushed past Kitty, though looking perhaps a shade more conscious: "Maybe we could go somewhere first for a drink?" This too, however, produced but a gaze of disapproval and a silence, bitter and vague, from Kitty.

Kitty seemed on the point of saying something harsh, but suddenly expressed herself otherwise. "You will regret this," she finally managed. "Do you suppose I will sit back and let you do this?"

Mary locked her arm around David's and they walked out of the house for an evening of celebration.

Kitty stood in silence with clenched fists and surging rage.

45

Mary realized that David was becoming to her the whole world, and more than the world, almost her hope of heaven. He stood between her and every thought of blind faith that in the past had kept her from her just freedom, as an eclipse intervenes between man and the bright sun. She felt comfortable in her recognition that she no longer needed to see God, for He had offered his angel to her and in that her salvation.

They arrived a little late at the restaurant in the piazza but the owner had held their reservation, for when David had called to make it, he had asked for the most expensive champagne in the house. After seating Maria, David left to have a word with the owner and as he returned, her eyes were eagerly searching for him. He smiled as he approached her, and she saw his face luminous, his big brown eyes smiling, tenderness and passion in every lineament. She quailed momentarily—then she rallied. Then something unexpected happened. She stood up and moved towards him to embrace him. Passionate scene, daring demonstration: she must be prepared—she whetted her lips. As he reached her, she asked herself silently, "Will he kiss me?"

David lifted his hand and lovingly moved a rebellious lock of hair that, caught in the moving air, was dancing on her face. In doing so his fingertips caressed her cheek and she trembled with excitement. He then cupped her face in his hands like one carefully puts his hands together to hold water. She closed her eyes and awaited judgment on her prayers. She felt his warm breath on her face just before she felt the gentle pressure of his warm lips on hers. Time stood still. The sweetness of the kiss began, moment by moment, to melt away the bitterness and suffering of her past years.

A curious feeling of elation surged through her and she felt as if she was seventeen again, young, innocent and vulnerable. Most of all vulnerable, and she liked it. Tears of joys gathered in her closed eyes and rolled down her cheeks to rest on her lips, quivering with ecstasy. In the salty taste of her tears David's lips burned with passion and she responded by putting both her arms around his waist and pressing her trembling body hard against his. The music of romance and passion rose to her heart and in its wild beating there was no limit she was not prepared to cross. In his embrace her soul took flight and soured high above in the unblemished sky, giving fuel to her vulnerability. So this was love; she was summoned to behold a revelation. She felt a remorseless slow, soft and sweet pang that left her languid. She was free in her soul, finally.

David's mind was blank, finally reaching that state of suspension where healing begins. His memories of the tor-turous past began to fade as a wave ebbs into an ocean. He wanted to take every moment of what he was experiencing and turn them all into a foundation on which he wanted to build his new life. He had wondered when their friendship would lead to closeness but he had never expected it to be so sudden, so soon. He was overcome with joy.

The setting sun as if with a sigh of pleasure dusted the western sky with its venetian-golden hue. He walked her towards an outside table close to the stage where music and dance were to be performed this evening. He wanted to immerse himself in a sphere of epicurean delight. Everything enchanted him.

The piazza began to fill with locals and tourists alike, but it was not too busy, for the event was not well advertised. The music and performance of dancers started while Mary and David enjoyed an evening of culinary delight with the most expensive champagne the restaurant offered. From where they were sitting they could watch the performance on stage and hear the music clearly. They sat side by side, watching the show as though they had been cast by the tempest on some deserted shore.

It was a strange dance, lilting, and changing as the music changed. But it had a dignity, intimate, passionate, yet never hurried, never violent, always becoming more intense. Maria seemed fascinated by the dance. He watched her. Her child-like indifference to consequences touched him with a sense of the disappearing distance between them. He wanted to play with the delicious warm surface of life, but felt checked by the relentless mass of cold beneath—the mass of life that has no sympathy with the individual, no cognizance of him as the new David.

As the night progressed so did the intensity of the music and the women dancers' faces transformed to a transported marvel; they were in the very cadence of glee. The quartet of musicians, in their fancy caps and their red velvet cloaks, made a music that came quicker and quicker, the dance grew faster and more intense, yet passionate in its intensity. The men seemed to fly and the women, drifting and palpitating, spun as if their souls resonated to a wind that was rushing upon them, through them.

The music came to a climax, the women gyrated their bodied. The dance passed into a possession, the men moved their feet faster, caught up the women and swung them from the platform, leapt with them for a second, and then the next phase of the dance began.

The quartet stood up now and poured their heart and soul into their music, a rhythm within a rhythm, a subtle approaching, drawing nearer to a climax again. Then once more the slow, intense, nearer movement of the dance began, always nearer, always to a more perfect climax.

The women waited and so did Maria, as if harmoniously in transport to the climax, when they would be cast into a movement surpassing all movement. The moment came when they were flung, borne away, lifted like a kite soaring on a powerful thermal, into the zenith and nave of the heavens, consummate.

Suddenly the dance came almost to an end, and the dancers stood in a circle, in the center of which was the most powerful male dancer, inconceivably vigorous in body, his dancing almost perfect. With every muscle in his body supple as steel, as strong as thunder, and yet so quick, so delicately swift, it was perfect. He was like a god, a strange yet natural phenomenon, most intimate and compelling. As the music suddenly built its pitch, he lifted in his arms the most delicate, the most beautiful female dancer; she dressed as a butterfly, her movements sensuous and seductive, a dance of virgin to the god of love. He threw her in the air spinning, the climax, the ecstasy, a sense of a great strength, crouching, ready to catch her. The violins swelled and quavered on the last notes, he caught her midair and she sank to a crumpled butterfly on the stage, as a great burst of applause filled the piazza.

Oh, to fall in love like that, to the languorous magic melody of such a tune. The last dance by the artists of the dance troupe, before the public was asked to take the floor for dancing, was a sensuous performance by beautifully sculpted male and female dancers, as the cellos sighed to the musical moon.

46

Upon the horizon a big, a gigantic, blinding white shard of glass from a broken cosmic window danced in the sky, insubstantial yet overwhelmingly powerful. It added extra magic to an enchanted evening. Mary closed her eyes, moved by the lingering music, the moon, the wine and sumptuous feast, and offered once again her lips as a gesture of love and friendship to David. David leaned forward and then their lips brushed like young wild flowers in the wind. Her old world seemed to be crumbling as if constructed of sand—shaky, ambiguous, and impermanent. Her new world in which none of the old rules, the old taboos, applied, was evolving. In her heart and soul, she was free.

A velvety darkness with silvery half crystalline, half misty sky suited the melodious music lingering on the piazza and the night felt pleasant and vibrant with rich tension. David looked at Maria and felt her love for him, but it was burdensome and painful to be so loved. Yes, it was a strange and awkward sensation for he did not want her family to be unhappy about it. On his way to see Maria he had decided that all his hopes rested on her, he expected to be rid of at least part of his suffering, and now, when all her heart turned towards him, he suddenly felt that he was immeasurably happier than before.

As slow and inviting music started to play, they found themselves dancing, holding each other closer, their hot breath arousing their inner desires. Her eyes were somehow too blue and their expression somehow too loving and unwavering. There was something inviting in that beautiful face, so young and vulnerable. And he was swept off full sail on the sea of dreams and hope. She looked up at him with eyes clear and transcendent as the heavens. There was a faint gleam of rapt light in her eyes. Her sensual beauty mesmerized David for she was his perfect Tuscan Dream. She was his Italian goddess. He pressed his body against hers and she offered no resistance.

Maria was a young, powerful, passionate woman, and she was unsatisfied body and soul. Her soul's satisfaction became a bodily dissatisfaction that screamed for salvation tonight. Her blood was heavy, excited, anarchic, insisting on her absolute right to satisfaction. She wanted freedom from her past, her oppressors, from her own mind. She wanted to act without thinking, deliberating or wondering what the world would say. She was listening not to the world tonight but only to her own inner voice.

And he gave her a feeling of vivid bliss, a happiness that gleamed like phosphorescence. There was completeness about him, about the perfect world he inhabited, which excluded sadness. It was final, defined. There was no yearning, no vague merging off into mistiness. He was clear and fine as solid rock, as a gleaming substance in moonlight. He seemed like a crystal that has achieved its perfected shape and has nothing more to achieve.

And then, when she was tipsy with bliss, her inner voice began to talk to her. In him was a steady flame burning, burning, a flame of the heart, of the spirit, something new and pure that held the soft, sensuous Maria in submission, besides all the doubts that had once occupied her mind. Tonight she felt free to surrender and in her surrender find her triumph.

Her love was wild as Africa; her desires were like the whirlwinds of the desert, whose torrid expanse was in her eyes, the azure, love-laden desert, with its changeless skies, its cool and starry nights. A love without possession is maintained by the exasperation of desire, but there comes a moment when all suffering within us is evaporated in a flash. This was that moment and Maria and David were in its carefree bliss.

She glanced at him again, with unchanging eyes. To her he was a piece of the heavens. Her world was absolute, without consciousness of self. In her universe he was a tall, dark and handsome stranger, a foreign signore. She was carefree, candid and open as the skies. Only a determination of the will appeared, as if to surrender to him.

She, dancing with her cheek caressing his, whispered, "What do you see when you look at me?" David in their champagne-induced bliss, whispered back in her ear, "Aphrodite, the queen of the senses, she, born of the sea-foam, is the luminousness of the gleaming senses, the phosphorescence of the sea. The senses become a conscious aim unto themselves. She is the gleaming morning, she is the luminous light, she is goddess of creation, her white, cold fire consumes me and then gives me new life. That is you, just like the fresco on your bedroom ceiling."

"More," she whispered, pressing her cheek against his, "say more, David. You know me so well."

"You are the very soul of the Italian since the Renaissance. You can do anything you want. I want to bask in the sunshine with you, gathering up desire into our veins, which in the night we will distil into ecstatic sensual delight, the intense, white-hot ecstasy of sensual bliss and moonlight that will consume us, fuse us into one. We were meant to be together."

Her eyes were light blue, reflecting the silver brightness of the full moon, showing the fibrils like a purple-veined flower at twilight, and somehow, mysteriously, joy seemed to quiver in the iris. She swooned in a kind of intense bliss. He saw the silver of two tears, tears of happiness for she held a smile in the moonlit ivory of her face. His heart tightened with tenderness, and he laughed then bent to kiss her. She kissed him back and their bodies remained entwined, burning with desire.

There were a million stars on such a clear, cold night, and they trickled so far down the horizon that they seemed to nestle between the tree branches like tiny Christmas lights. "Look there," said David, making up his own constellation, "there is the heart constellation." He then laughed at his feeble creativity and Mary laughed with him. The mystery of the night was intoxicating, inspiring desire.

"It is the first communion of love," she whispered in his ear. "Yes, I now share your happiness and sorrow. Our souls are united in love. To love, even without hope, is happiness. Ah, no man on earth could give me a joy equal to that of having your arms around me, I am truly happy tonight. I accept my destiny and am happy to give myself to you with no reservation. I will be to you that which you will me to be."

He wished to kiss her hands for he remembered that was where it all started. She trembled, then pushed her body close against his, and whispered again in a voice of entreaty: "Would you take me? I am yours tonight; tonight I shall be simply a thing of yours, and tomorrow I will wake up in your arms a new woman."

He gazed at her with an ecstasy that should have been contagious. She trembled in his arms slightly and stopped to stare deep into his eyes with her mesmerizing blue ones. He was filled with bliss by these words, mingled with the warmth of her love—a combination which gives to women so great a power of persuasion, they know how and when to give freely.

"Let us go to your place." She was blinding with sheer joy. David settled the bill and they left the restaurant to walk to his place, beyond her house, only a short distance away. As they approached her house she put her arms around his neck and after a soft kiss on his lips said, "You go on and wait for me. I will be along in a few minutes for I would like to dress up in something quite special for you, for tonight. Have soft music and low lights and perhaps a little more champagne."

He was in a trance, his consciousness seeming suspended. "Si la mia signora," said David to her, quiet, almost invisible or inaudible, as it seemed, like a spirit addressing her. "Don't keep me waiting," he kissed her back and told her to come straight up to his room that he intended to leave unlocked and, whistling some old tune, sauntered over to his place to make sure he had more chilled champagne for to-night. The moon was shining above the river and sprinkling its magic; it was the night for lovers.

47

They were both by nature intensely passionate. But the lines of their passion were opposite. Hers was the embryonic, refined, emotional and discriminating, but wanting to mix and mingle with someone of fiery passion. That was David, a man of burning passion. His was the hard, clear, vulnerable force of the heart, fine things and nature. She was the flint and he the steel. But they waited for a spark, the all-consuming fire, which was a third thing, belonging to neither of them, at least not yet. He was still hungry and full of desire. He was much younger than she.

Moonlight filtering through drawn curtains provided a romantic ambiance to David's room. The soft music and candlelight intoxicated his mood already heady with the champagne. His ecstasy brought dreams unspeakable, which fed his imagination, fostered his susceptibilities, and strengthened his intent. He had often attributed those sublime desires to the cupid charged with molding his spirit to its divine destiny, endowing his soul with the aptitude of seeing beauty in everything, preparing his heart for the magic that makes a man a poet.

And then came the moment he had been waiting for. He heard the door open and close, and she blew the candle out. David moved over in his bed to make room for her and whispered, "Let me see you, I would love to see you in your natural beauty, shimmering in the candlelight."

"Shh," she whispered by putting her soft lips close to his ear and then squeezing it between her wet lips and tugging at his earlobe to excite his desire. He kissed her on her lips as she lay close to him with her arms around him. Swooning with her entrancing perfume and his increasing desire for her, his body in hot flames seemed to have subdued all his other senses except to become one with her.

He kissed her forehead, her eyelids and her lips. She in the dim light felt his face with her hands and then moved his lips to her neck and then down to her breasts. David liked her uncharacteristic boldness for she was reborn with renewed confidence, and so he let her take charge. She with expert hands undressed David and then allowed him to free her from her smooth satin dress, keeping a silk scarf around her neck as if for modesty, or to spice up the play.

She guided him around her body, in total control and he in ecstasy. Their bodies moved in unison as if playing to a rhythm, making him all-powerful, a man, as she expertly gyrated her hips under him. He was breathing heavily as his heart raced with excitement and she let out a little moan. It was not an animal passion. It was sensuality but sharp and searing as fire, burning the soul to tinder. Burning out the inhibitions in the most secret places. She responded to his desires and let him have his way and his will of her. She had to be a passive, consenting thing, like a slave, a physical slave. Yet the passion licked 'round her, consuming, and she let out a peal of laughter like pearls bouncing off a marble floor.

A laugh not of ecstasy but more of victory.

Suddenly it was as if a thousand volts went through his body. His mind equated something horrific in a matter of seconds—jasmine perfume, bold demeanor, expert hands and that laugh. He reached out and put the bedside table lamp on and what he saw left him dumbfounded. While he reeled in shock, Kitty laughed out loud. She sat up in bed and mockingly said, "I told you I would never let you hurt Mary. She will never want you now, not after I tell her all about us, lover boy." Her laughter became louder and was now sinister.

A strange and violent feeling stirred in the pit of his stomach and transformed as it rose into a piercing cry, loud like that of a wounded animal. The night—its silence—its rest, was rent in twain by this savage, severe, piercing sound. His pulse suddenly stopped. His heart stood still, the whole world around him faded. He interlaced his fingers and cradled his spinning head. With the heels of his palms, he squeezed hard to put pressure on his temples to release the agony he was feeling from a bursting head. The cry died, and was not renewed. Indeed, whatever made him utter that fearful scream could not soon repeat it: He felt paralyzed as consternation took control.

David felt sharp pain and tightening in his chest as if someone was squeezing his heart, pulling it out of his chest. His fists were tightly clenched, his fingers closed over his thumbs, which were pressed bloodless. Suddenly he felt something tight within him give way. He exhaled. He was finished with being cheated of what was his destiny. Anger never felt so light and lovely. He was strong and full of animal life, but aimless, as though his wits scarcely controlled him.

Something inside him snapped and he heard Kitty struggling for air as his vice-like grip around her throat tightened. As she struggled, scratching his face with her fingernails in a futile fight for her life, he said in a low and harsh voice, "If you wish to go on a journey of revenge then plan on digging two graves. I am going to end your games forever. You will never bother Maria again."

A rustle and the door opened. Horror-struck, Maria let out a smothered cry. "David, what have you done?" She turned and vanished and in a state of confusion, David relaxed his grip and Kitty coughed violently. David ran after Maria, shouting her name, but she was gone. He ran out in the street but saw no sign of her. In an agony of trepidation he looked down the road…then turned around and looked back…and a sinking feeling gripped his heart.

He jogged towards the piazza but apart from a few late-night tourists it was empty. He hurried towards the railway station, for Mary had once told him that when she got upset, she found the old building peaceful and soothing. He looked around the station but Maria had disappeared. *Think, think*, he said to himself. *No, she would not return to her house, but where would she go?* He slowly sank onto a bench outside the station and buried his head in his hands. *Where should I go? What shall I do? Oh, God, it cannot end like this. Why?*

His mind was in a whirl and unable to put together any coherent thought, as he was trembling all over from a sort of wild hysterical sensation, in which there was a strong element of insufferable pain. He felt fatigue wash over him. His face was twisted as after a fit. Any thought of something redeemable, any slight positive sensation stimulated and revived his energies at once, but such feelings evaporated in a flash and his strength failed as quickly as the stimulus died.

He had lost sense of time and had no idea how long he had been sitting there. Suddenly he was startled as someone tapped on his shoulder. It was Affonso talking to him with a couple of Carabiniere standing behind him, "David Hawthorne, I am arresting you for the murder of Kitty Zuccato. You have the right to remain silent. Anything you say can and will be used against you in a court of law. You have the right to an attorney present during questioning. If you cannot afford an attorney, one will be appointed for you. Do you understand these rights?"

"What?" He looked around as if he did not know where he was, "Dead, Kitty? No, no, no, she was quite alive when I left her."

"So you do admit to being with her in your hotel room?"

"Of course, but it was a mistake. We had an argument and I shook her a bit but she cannot be dead, I did not strangle her. She was alive when I left her."

"So you were with her and there was a struggle and you did not kill her but did try to strangle her?" Affonso was taking notes as the Carabiniere cuffed him and dragged him to the waiting patrol car. By the time they arrived at the police station, the gravity of the situation David was in began to sink in and he then realized that he had been charged with the murder of Kitty and not just by anyone but by Affonso, who had so dearly loved her. He sat in an interrogation room with his head hung low in anticipation of pending doom; there was no way out of this nightmare. He realized that he should not have signed the statement he gave of accidently sleeping and subsequently fighting with Kitty and in a rage trying to strangle her. It now dawned on him that he had signed his own death warrant.

48

The next morning when he woke up in his cell after only a couple of hours of fitful sleep, he was told he had a visitor. Still in an utterly chaotic state of mind, he tried to recall where he was and what had happened during the previous night, and so gazed at the prison guard curiously. He rose to his feet, looked 'round in wonder, as though surprised at finding himself in this place, and went towards the guard. He was exhausted in every limb, but also both agitated and angry. He was crushed and even humiliated. He could have laughed at himself in his anger as a dull animal rage boiled within him.

The guard gestured him to follow and escorted him to a waiting room where Maria was waiting for him

"Oh, David," she cried. "What did happen last night?"

David took a long and searching look at her and slowly the events of the previous night began to unfold in his mind, but a completely expected and exceedingly simple question perplexed and bitterly confounded him.

"You…" and his voice trailed off. He lowered his head and slowly rubbed his forehead with the palm of his hand. He raised his eyes again and retried, "You came to see me. You're not upset?"

She looked at him with moist eyes and responded, "Of course I am upset, David, I lost my baby sister. But I'm sure it was a tragic accident, Kitty played terrible games with both of us."

David's voice broke and he seemed unable to articulate the words clearly. "What are you saying? You think I killed her?" He looked at her wide-eyed, trying in his own mind to piece together the events of the fateful evening.

"David," she paused and then lowered her voice so it was only audible to David. "When I arrived at your place your door was open and I saw you and Kitty fighting. I heard her mocking you with how she tricked you into sleeping with her to make me give you up and when that made you violent and you started strangling her. It was as if my world had come to an end. The hotel owner heard screams, found her body and reported it to the police. But what you did was due to sheer provocation that resulted in an accidental death and I will vouch for it in court, if necessary. I will wait for you. They cannot keep you here for too long."

David kept shaking his head in disagreement as Maria tried to console him and finally he, in an exasperated tone, said, "But Mary, I did not kill her. I swear; she was quite alive when I left her. There is something sinister afoot and we must try to find the truth. Yes, I hurt her, but please, you have to believe me that I did not kill her."

"I do believe you, David. If you say you did not kill her then you did not kill her. I think we should get your father to come for I think we need his help."

"No, no, I don't want my dad involved again. If you are with me and believe me then that is all I need. We can fight it together."

"We cannot, David. You know how Affonso felt about Kitty and how he dislikes you. He is going to make this personal to ensure he puts you away for good. I cannot lose you, David. Let me contact your father and I will explain everything. I am sure he will believe me. Please, let's ask for his help."

David mulled it over for a few moments and the gravity of the situation he was in began to sink in, especially when he thought of Affonso. "Okay, but let me explain it to him. Oh, Maria," he closed his eyes and rubbed his face with the palms of his hands, "I cannot believe what has happened. But I am pleased that you believe me. I am so happy to see you here."

The prison guard interrupted, declaring that visiting time was up, and escorted David back to his cell.

Soon after, David asked to place a call to his dad in England. Affonso came to visit him and stood outside his cell, glowering down at him with a derisive smile flickering on his lips. Affonso, who had made his way up from insignificance, was morbidly given to self-admiration, and had the highest opinion of his intelligence and capacities.

"This time," a haughty smile appeared on his lips, "you are mine. You want to call your father and want him here to be humiliated, then be my guest. But my advice to you is to forget about your father and ask for forgiveness. Plead for mercy so the judge goes easy on you." He wore a huge ring with a precious stone in it and he slowly twirled it around his finger as he continued to stare at David as if immensely enjoying the moment. "I hope you rot here for the rest of your life." He banged hard his truncheon on the metal grill door, turned around and left.

The following morning David's father was at the visitor's room of the prison with the same attorney he had hired before. This defense attorney did not come cheap but was considered the best in Florence, if not in all of Italy. The attorney told David that he would like to talk with him alone after he had spoken with his father and would be waiting outside.

David had expected his father to be sympathetic and supportive and he was not disappointed.

Questioning with his eyes, his lips parted to utter a question, his father was unable to form words. He let out a sigh of exasperation then said, "Son, I won't mince words with you. No matter what gulf exists between us, you're my son and I will do anything to protect you. But I cannot let you die a coward's death. You were the best as a soldier, still are and always will be. It is in our blood." He looked intently at David's still face. "And whether you like it or not, life goes on. If there is anything that I will take to my grave as certain, it is that life continues. Don't let the emotions of women mislead you for they know nothing about the life of a man as a soldier. It isn't true that whatever doesn't kill you only makes you stronger—sometimes you are left as little more than the most fragile, defenseless shadow of the person you once were, broken and insubstantial and weak and lost. But whatever doesn't kill you does leave you vulnerable to another day. Fight. Fight back. Your life—or what's left of it—will go on. That is not always necessarily a good thing, not if you don't fight for what is yours."

"Dad," David answered, not happy being given a military lecture, "I do appreciate your coming over and I am sorry for what happened, but I am no longer a soldier or fighting anyone's war."

"You talk like this because you didn't stay back in the Falklands long enough to have the sweet taste of victory. The magnificence of our nation lies in the glory of our victories on the war front. Our brave men laid their lives down. Your brother gave his life to make our nation great. Their victory will always be celebrated, now and forever. What on earth are you doing here and what do you have against a life of glory?"

"Huh, the glory of being victorious fails to tell the story of the tears and anguish of loved ones whose sons, brothers, and fathers lost their lives fighting bravely." David's voice held a tinge of irritation for he detested any talk that glorified wars.

"Ah, but the sweet taste of victory you can only appreciate when you liberate a nation from oppression and wipe out the enemy." David's father's chest expanded and his voice found firmness as he tried to engage David in his favorite subject.

"Oh, please, Dad," David shook his head in dismay. "Contrary to popular belief in tales of war heroes and their great bravado, a battle zone only gives a human being a sense of his weakness and insignificance. It is not a fight against an enemy or a struggle for liberation. It is killing someone you suddenly come upon face-to-face, for if you didn't then he would kill you. You learn to kill without remorse and for no good reason. Before you become a hero, you must become an angel of death."

He shook his head vigorously and added, "Dad, please, what are you doing? Leave this ugly topic for some other time. Once again, thanks for being here. Let me speak with the attorney now and then I will talk with you again. Where are you staying, anyway?"

"Oh, don't bother about me. I will visit with the attorney after you and then see you. Stay strong, son, you'll be okay. No son of mine is a murderer and we'll prove your innocence. We have the best to fight for you."

He contemplated for a moment and then hesitantly said, "I never liked your mother's idea of sending you away all alone to countries you know nothing about. Anyway, I am here now and I'll take care of everything. I'll show these Italians what Scots are made of. But you don't look pleased, aren't you relieved that I'm here?"

He should, if he had deliberated, have replied to this question by saying something conventionally vague and polite, but the answer somehow slipped from his tongue before he was aware—"It is not a matter of being pleased, Dad, and it is not about you. It is about me, my life."

Neither man at that moment had any idea of the brewing tempest that was going to charter a new direction for David's life.

49

The chief prosecutor was convinced that there was compelling evidence to go to trial to try David for the murder of Kitty Zuccato. Police under the command of Affonso had put together an extensive array of evidence, first to discredit David, and then to establish a motive for murder. Several eyewitness accounts established that David was dating both sisters, separately of course. He was often seen having lunches with Kitty and either breakfasts or dinners with Mary. Additionally, he had been seen going for walks alongside the Arno River with Mary. Several witnesses verified seeing David often hanging around the Zuccato house and at times going in to see the family.

Although information from his past case where he was implicated and later cleared for the murder of Antonio was not allowed to be directly used in the current case, the police in a subtle maneuver did produce a report where they showed that David had a short temper as evident from his fight in the bar and later in front of the Zuccato house, where Antonio was found dead. The police also dug up what they could on David's military career and found that he was trained in hand-to-hand combat and had killed many people during the Falkland war.

Having clearly established that David could fly off the handle, was courting both sisters, and trained to kill, the police came up with an interesting and compelling angle for the motive. In their meticulous search, they found an incriminating link between the murders of Antonio and Kitty—the rare and invaluable pendant. On that fateful night, as confirmed by Mary, Kitty was wearing the pendant and when the police found the body it was gone. Later the medical examiner in his postmortem report indicated that Kitty had bruising around her neck that would support the theory that a chain was yanked off her neck.

The police also got a statement from the shop owner in Sienna that David had brought Kitty and her pendant to the shop and was keenly interested in finding out its worth. Although, like the last time, the pendant was once again not recovered, this time its retrieval was not critical in charging David with the crime. The reason for this was the statement made by David himself, admitting that he was at the scene of murder, fighting with Kitty over sex and then strangling her. David's fingerprints were matched with the bruising imprints on Kitty's neck, leaving no doubt the strangulation was the cause of death and that David's hands had applied the pressure around her neck.

Both the police and public prosecutor were quite convinced that they had undeniable and extensive evidence which would convict David of the murder of Kitty Zuccato and result in a sentence of life. But the defense attorney was not yet satisfied that everything had been looked into in fine detail, and until such time that he had personally considered and evaluated all options, he was not ready to make his case.

One day during visiting hours, while David's father was waiting for David, Affonso approached him in the waiting room and in a low but contemptuous tone said, "Go home, old man, your son is never coming home."

Coming in from his cell, David saw his father shudder: A singularly marked expression of disgust, anger, and hatred warped his countenance almost to distortion. Since he knew his father's temper, he quickly walked over to him and said, "Dad, let's sit over there, and never mind his threat. Like the last time, they have nothing but circumstantial evidence and besides, they cannot prove any of it."

David's father pursed his lips as if he had trouble sharing David's confidence. As they sat in the supervised visitor's room, his father said, "I wish you had not come to Italy and fallen in love with a foreign woman. This is a strange country and Italians are odd people. The Italian people are called 'Children of the Sun.' They might better be called 'Children of the Shadow.' Their souls are dark and nocturnal. Do you realize that the situation you have fallen into could get you killed?"

David articulated, "I have never known anyone like her, and can hardly imagine anyone more unlike myself, yet from our very first meeting a strong feeling of love and understanding established itself between us." He paused in his reflection and stood. He found it hard to fix his mind on anything at that moment. He longed to forget himself altogether, to forget everything, and then to wake up and begin life anew.

The supervising guard looked at him, gesturing for him to sit down and, with his finger on his lips, to keep it down, but otherwise was without the slightest interest. He was a particularly unkempt person, in a place where many emotions flowed, and he obviously could not be bothered, as it had all become routine for him.

"Hell, I was ready to be killed for a lot less," David said with a faint smile on his face and a voice that showed unyielding conviction in his beliefs. "She is my reason for living and her love is worth dying for. Mother taught me that life is an ultimate gift and worth living, and birth at its beginning and death at its end are simply a measure of its length. It is not how long one might live. It is what one lives for. I don't believe in heaven and hell, but I do believe now in angels, for I am in love with one. A man can hold hope if he can love."

"What nonsense are you talking?" David's father frowned and waved his hand as if brushing all such thoughts away. He added, "You better stay focused, for this time it is not going to be as easy as the last." David's father moved to the edge of his seat and in a contemplative voice said, "Something I need to say to clear the air between us. You are in a serious and dangerous situation here and I don't want to lose you, for you are my only child alive, and your mother needs you, too. I know we have had differences in the past and I know you carry resentments because of the way I had treated your mother, but you need to get over it and bury our past and work with me to see you through this tough time. Now, I have heard everything you had to say about this Italian woman you seem to love, but we need a plan, are you willing to do what I ask?"

As David looked up at his dad, the sun appeared momentarily in the part of the sky that filled the window, the one located behind his dad, the circle half lit and half overcast. It seemed to throw one reluctant, dreary glance, and buried itself again instantly in the deep drift of cloud. The wind over the metal roof poured out a wild, melancholy wail. It was sad to hear, and David's mind momentarily ran off to his childhood when he and his younger brother used to play in the woods nearby their country home. Suddenly he missed his late brother. A puerile tear dimmed his eye while he continued to look at the window for the sun to reappear from behind the clouds—a tear of disappointment and impatience. Ashamed of it, he wiped it away. He lingered while his dad waited for him to respond, the sun now shutting itself wholly within darkening and dense clouds. The day grew dreary; rain came driving fast on the gale, a sign of approaching winter.

David needed his father on the outside to help him, but was not sure if he was willing to pay the price, afraid of what his father might ask. In a level tone he uttered, "Just because I explained the way I feel towards Maria, and you heard it all, doesn't necessarily mean you have listened to everything. And even if you have, there is no guarantee that you feel the way I do, so forgive me if I find it difficult to put the past behind and move on just because you say so. You never understood me before and you don't understand me now."

He saw his father's face stiffen but ignoring it, he continued, "I am trying to, as you say, clear the air between us. Don't get me wrong, I'm appreciative of your coming out and helping me, but Dad, it can't be and won't be all on your terms. You must first consider my feelings, okay?"

"You were born with clenched fists." Suddenly he smiled and added, "I always knew you as a stubborn child. Okay, we will work together." He paused for a moment and David let the momentarily silence between them linger. Rubbing his chin, David's father in an appealing but firm voice said, "Look son, I know you are being strong, but times like these call for tougher measures. I listened to you, okay, and I've now heard everything you've to say. We will deal with whatever is bothering you about your past, but there is a time for it and that is not now. I am sorry for bringing it up before. Now, you must trust me that I am here for you. I am here because I care for you and I want to get you away from this place."

David's father then talked about the ongoing investigation the defense attorney had undertaken to unravel any hidden facts that may yet surface, for he was known for his uncanny ability to read between the lines of police and medical examiner's reports. And he had something up his sleeve that he had not yet fully shared with David that just might get David acquitted of all alleged charges.

Book IV
Florence, Italy

Winter 1983
"Better the cold fury of winter than the scorching breath of
a pursuing devil."

50

One early afternoon on a cold wintery day, the defense attorney came to see David, and unlike on his previous visits, there was something quite different in his eyes and countenance. In his usual philosophical fashion he said to David, "The calm before a storm offers an opportunity to prepare, and those who fall into complacency offered by that calm have no one but themselves to blame when hit by the wrath of the storm. You understand what I am saying?"

"I think so, but I'm not sure," David replied, wrinkling his forehead.

"David," the attorney said in a mysterious tone, "think very hard before you answer my question for I have found something that may change the whole complexion of this case."

David focused on his face and showed his attentiveness by simply nodding. The attorney with his piercing eyes looked into David's liquid brown eyes and said, "We know those were your fingerprints on Kitty's neck and you admitted that at one point you had squeezed her neck. But once again, according to your testimony, you did not kill her for when you left the room she was still alive. Right?"

"That is right," David spoke in rote fashion, for he had given this information so many times that he wondered what new grounds the attorney might have found.

"Did you at any time," he moved closer to David, "did you at any time, and think before you answer, try to strangle her with the scarf that they found on her body?"

"No." David's voice was firm and he answered instantly, for he did not have to think about his answer. "I remember the dainty little scarf for that was the only thing she had on her body, but there was no way I did anything with the scarf."

The attorney leaned back in his chair and suddenly a smile broke out on his lips and there was a twinkle in his eyes. "David, I went back to the medical examiner and we went over Kitty's postmortem report again in great detail. The police conveniently ignored one little remark that apart from the bruises on Kitty's neck caused by your hands and by ripping off her pendant necklace, there is a very deep bruise that could have only been caused if someone used something like a scarf to strangle her. The medical examiner could not be sure what resulted in the ultimate death, strangulation by your hands or by the scarf."

Listening carefully, David waited for a moment or two, but when he saw that the attorney had concluded his new findings, in a perplexed voice he said, "So, if the medical examiner is not sure, then how can this help us?"

"Well, you see," he leaned forward and with a broadening smile said, "as long as he is not sure then there is doubt and the public prosecutor has to prove his case without a reasonable doubt. So we have a breach that we could exploit. Remember the missing pendent? We would submit to the judge that when the perpetrator found Kitty alone, for he must have stalked her like he did with Antonio, he struggled with her to snatch away her pendant. She put up a fight, perhaps in her delirium thinking it was still you trying to strangle her, and he found the scarf which he used to strangle her. Then he ripped the necklace off her neck and disappeared once again the same way as he did before. After all, we do know that there is a party who was keen on possessing the two rare coins. And guess what? This party as I have discovered has some unsavory connections, for it is closely related to the mafia."

David looked at the attorney, thinking if that was all they had, then they would need divine intervention. He did not want to discourage the attorney so adopted silence as his best support to the man's theory. The attorney, getting up from his chair, said to David, "I want you to go over and over in your head the night Kitty died, and try to recall if you saw anyone who was following you or watching you at the dance. Do you remember, you told me about the shopkeeper in Sienna who has a cousin in Florence who wanted to acquire the two coins? Did you ever meet with him? If you come up with anything, let me know immediately, for the court date is approaching, okay?"

David nodded in the affirmative and the attorney left. That evening Maria came to visit David and he informed her of the new development. Maria was even less convinced than David that such a theory would hold water in the court. She wondered if pleading guilty and cooperating with the authorities might lessen the sentence but at that, David declared, "No way, Maria. How could you even suggest such a thing? I think there is a strong similarity between Antonio and Kitty's deaths: the pair of rare coins. Somehow we need to convince the police to investigate that cousin of the Sienna shopkeeper who so persistently tried to acquire them."

"The police and especially Affonso are after your blood. Why can't we make a deal and get you off the hook with a lighter sentence? I will wait for you, David. I have waited already for several years. Another few will not change anything. This way at least we know we can be together one day. Why do you feel such an arrangement would be so terrible?" Her arms went up in a desperate supplication. It wasn't pleading, it was asking a question.

"Because, Maria, I'm innocent. You do believe me, don't you?" David looked into her big blue eyes and saw bewilderment, panic, and despair. He was puzzled. Something was ebbing out of her, some vitality moved away, leaving her wounded. What was it?

She remained quiet so David tried to reassure her of his love for her. "Yesterday, I walked a little in the prison yard during an exercise hour, thinking of you, and I beheld you in imagination so near me, I scarcely missed your actual presence. I thought of the life that lay before me—your life, Maria—an existence more expansive and stirring than my own. I wondered why your grandmother foresaw my life to be in ruins due to our companionship, as for me it blossomed like a rose. I'm happy, Maria. I truly am. For the first time in my life I know what real love can offer because I have you and your love in my life."

"There is something inside me that knows beyond every rational and irrational doubt," Maria said, whispering as if imparting a secret to David, "that I was not meant to walk alone. And I feel deep in my heart that He longs to stand beside me. There is a verse in Matthew that says, 'Ask and it will be given to you, seek and you will find, knock and the door will be opened to you.' I know that my prayers will not go unanswered, for you and I were destined to be together, don't you see? But I'm afraid, afraid that if you plead innocence and Affonso is determined to put you away then maybe I will never see you again. But if your attorney and the chief prosecutor make a deal for you, pleading accidental death because of foul play on the part of Kitty, and I vouch for that, then maybe they will be lenient, Then you could be out in maybe five years or so and we could be together forever. Nobody could touch us then. I would go anywhere you want us to go to live our life peacefully. Can you not see logic in what I am saying? Why do you not accept it?"

David felt as if he was standing on the edge of a cliff with a strange compelling notion in his heart to jump off.

51

He didn't say anything for a while, just watched her as if he could glean the right response from the tilt of her head or the rosiness in her cheeks. Why was she so persistent that he plead guilty and what if the authorities put him away for the rest of his life, what would she do then? Wasn't it a big gamble she was betting on? There was a clue in her eyes that he could only half decipher but rather than conjure a manipulative way to win her confidence, he chose to go with his own feelings—to be open and honest. So he said, "To accept is to atone and I am not guilty." Seeing Maria disappointed by his remark, he tried to mollify her, "My life is like a long empty road as if from here to eternity, and I admit, I cannot see anything at the end of it. But I am willing to walk it just for the privilege of the trip for life is a journey, isn't that what they call it? And I would do anything to take this journey with you." Though his voice sounded upbeat he felt sad and even a trifle frightened, for he was well aware of a dark period that was staring him in the face.

"Look at me," she pleaded, squeezing his hands in hers. "Why don't you give me some of your sadness and in return take some of my happiness, for then you might be able to survive and then I could live too. And we would continue to survive in this fashion until such time you are free and until then, no matter how far apart we are, whenever you need me just reach out for me as far as you can and I will cover the rest of the distance."

David remained perplexed, he was asked to take a step in the simplest form of a question, but somehow he knew there was a greater meaning and he was supposed to understand it. His only hope was that with long silent pauses she would offer further information that may unravel the mystery she was weaving. He did not have to wait for long before Maria tried to explain again, "You may be the only person who would understand that the song we were brought together to sing remains unsung to this day. Our time has not yet come to pass and the words have not been rightly set; there is only the agony of wishing in my heart. The morning will surely come, the darkness will vanish, and we will be together one day. All I know is that I will have no sleep tonight or tomorrow or the day after that, for I will keep gazing on the far-away gloom of the sky, and my heart will wander wailing with the restless wind thinking of you, and of us."

There was a short-lived moment when something stirred in David's heart and he thought he was getting nearer to what she was asking for but then it faded and he failed to grasp her true intent. He could almost hear the cogs turning in her mind but felt frustrated. In an exasperated tone, he asked, "How would you find that freedom, the one you so crave, when I am locked up here? If I fight for my innocence and am let out as a free man, and I believe I can, for if you remember, I have been put through such a test before, then I could understand that true freedom would be attained by our being together." He asked the same question he had asked before in the hope that this time she would elaborate and offer a clearer picture.

Maria's gaze darted around the room as if she was feeling uncomfortable by either the question or her surroundings and then in a low voice articulated, "Freedom is all I want, all I ever wanted, but to even hope for it now I feel ashamed." She continued in a strained voice, "If I have made things more difficult," her voice was harsh with pain, "you will forgive me."

This was one of the cruel cuts of pain that love gives. Besides, David never knew how to handle the tears of a pretty woman. He smiled to lighten her mood as he stared at her innocent, plaintive lips, and her large eyes haunted with pain. "Forgive you?" he repeated. "Forgive you for my perfect happiness, the only real happiness I have ever known?"

This was a culminating point where the nature of things would change, but David was still not quite clear about her intent. It was the most complex byzantine labyrinth. "David," she said again. "I mean...I really love you. My love for you has no bounds and I would never let anything, anything at all hurt our love. What happened to Kitty, it happened for us to be together, do you understand?"

Two things happened then. A thought exploded through him like lightning charring a rotten tree: had providence shown him the way? Why could he not see before what Maria was saying? Something inside like a sudden spark evoked awareness in David's heart, making him realize that she was not pleading but confessing, confessing for what he now understood and it need not be uttered. Also, in a flash he knew what had to be done. She had made the ultimate sacrifice and now it was his turn to reciprocate.

David turned to her, his eyes warm and moist. "I love you, too, Maria," he said, his voice deep with emotion. "I'm sorry for acting like such an idiot. I do understand now what you are saying and thank you for your love, love no man is luckier than I am to have. You made a remarkable sacrifice for our love and I will do my part. I will not let you down, not let us down."

And even as she was grateful for his words, she was aware of her disappointment, of having betrayed herself. She knew that she had taken the easy way out; that she had let him down. What she had meant to say was not, "I love you," at all. What she had wanted to say was, "I love life," a self-declaration as naked and real as pain after a blow. And then, a door slammed shut somewhere in the inner recesses of Maria's mind. If she had said what she really intended to say, she knew David would not have understood. She must now live with her lie forever and hope he still respected her. A lonely feeling swept over her like an icy wind, and she shivered. She would now be alone for a long time.

She kept her silence for a minute while he waited, as if offering his reasons for letting her, for almost making her talk. What she herself wanted was not, for the second time, to cry, as it were, in public. She had never seen anything like the kindness showed by David, and she wished to do it justice, but she knew what she was about, and justice was not wronged by her being able to stick to her point, or at least, so she had convinced herself. She had lowered her voice to a deep depth, though speaking with a rich glibness, and David, after a sharp surprise, was already guessing the sense of her appeal.

Maria tightened her hands around his. She felt herself stinging with painful joy, but the supervising guard was studying her curiously. She leaned back in her place, closed her eyes and said, "Thank you, I'll wait for you, my love. You and I were two asymptotes bearing one towards the other, yet unable to meet. Fate miscarried all my attempts. But nothing will prevent us from being together after you come out. I will wait for you for as long as it takes."

David sat there looking at her hands, the most beautiful hands he had ever seen, those he had fallen in love with the first time he saw them, but his mind was miles away. His life would now take a different turn, one that he had not thought of before, or prepared for in order to understand his future. In a flash the pictures of his childhood, war experiences, the time in Florence and now this prison floated and intermingled in his mind.

He raised his head slowly and gazed into her eyes. There it was again, that sparkle in her eyes that compelled him to open his heart to her. He said, "I'm so sorry to have you go through all this. Everything I despised in my life turned into tools of vengeance to destroy all that I craved. I was never meant to be a soldier, a killing machine. I hate everything about my past because it was without you. I look forward to our days together." And just as slowly as he had raised his head earlier, he lowered it, lost in his thoughts.

Downcast eyes concealed his emotions and for Maria, they were like obliterated words of invisible ink on a blank sheet of paper, for the windows to his soul were closed. She got up and walked away without saying goodbye. She left him lost in his own world, lost in his past.

There was a sudden, brittle silence in the room.

52

When once more alone, back in his cell, David reflected on the decision he had committed himself to make a few moments ago. The purpose he had been yearning for all his life was now only a few short days away, for his court date was set up a week from now. Instead of fear he felt elation and was content, and took such feelings as support for the right decision. In the back of his mind his mother's words rang, "Dreams and hope are not fleeting fancy; they are built on many personal sacrifices. Don't waste your life looking for death for it will find you. Keep searching for what you desire, as it is the secret of living. Don't ever be afraid of pursuing your dreams."

As time passed, his soul began to expand, to exult, with the strangest sense of freedom and triumph he'd ever felt. It seemed as if an invisible bubble had burst, and that he had struggled out into unknown liberty. His feelings justified the decision he had committed himself to and he found himself unable to control his whirling mind to calmly evaluate the pros and cons of how his life may turn out. Tomorrow he would have a session with his attorney and dad to go over their strategy for the day of the trial. He wondered how they would react to his decision.

The next morning at dawn David looked towards the eastern sky through his small window, hoping to find a faint glow that would dissolve the darkness, but the sky remained dark, aided by murky clouds. Winter wasn't pretty in Florence. He wished that the winter sun would come up quickly. He wanted to rejoice in its warmth. He did not want the darkness to cloud his mind. The darkness, though thinning as clouds dispersed, seemed to hang on the fringes of the eastern horizon. Then, the yellow-orange globe, emerging on a vague horizon, propped its shivering cheek on the cool waters of Arno, making its westward journey towards the Tyrrhenian Sea at Marina di Pisa. It seemed to stop for a while, as if hesitant of its conviction until, with reluctant movement, the sun rose over the city, embracing the rapidly moving waters of the river, the red rooftops of the city and its ornate buildings and piazzas as it has done for centuries.

Soon David sank into a complete blankness of mind, but there was a light in his heart—perhaps even thought and intelligence, but also a gleam of something like folly.

Late in the morning when his dad and the defense attorney arrived, David sat across a table facing them with a firmness around his mouth and determined look in his eyes. Before either of them could utter a word he said, "Sometimes truth has multi-dimensional facets of facts and fiction. I know that the public prosecutor has an uncanny ability to intermingle these to make a statement to convict me of the alleged charges, but the game plan has changed. Now I've something that he cannot refute. I should have paid attention before to what you said about being brave and fighting for my freedom. I am ready to fight for what I believe in. Tomorrow comes with such promise that I don't know how to explain to you that there is no need to worry about the outcome."

David's father gave David's shoulder a reassuring squeeze. "Good," he whispered, but David's expression remained unyielding, as the atmosphere in the room was thick with unspoken words. David's father added, "I learned from my military career that one must persevere even though climbing the precipice is an arduous task, comparing to falling from it. The latter inflicts damaging injuries that may render you incapacitated for the rest of your living days." He then lowered his voice to add gravity to his statement and added, "Remember, son, destiny awaits those who sit back and choose not to try. Fortunes are for those who pursue opportunity with passion."

David heard him but did not listen for he couldn't imagine how his father would react to what he wanted to say. "Listen, Dad," he looked in turn at both his father and the attorney, "I don't believe we have a strong case and I've decided that the best course for me is to plead guilty to an accidental death in exchange for leniency."

The attorney and David's father exchanged perplexed glances in disbelief and it was David's father who spoke first. "David, I know you are scared but we must trust the ability of our attorney, he is the best in Italy and you know he has come through before. He is confident that we have a very strong case."

As David's father waited for a response to his plea the attorney said, "What made you change your mind? Is there something that I ought to know that you have not told us thus far?"

David rested both his arms on the table and explained, "I know I am not an attorney but I do understand that if we lose the case then they will crucify me on the charges of first-degree murder to the maximum extent of the law. The evidence against me is extensive but if I plead voluntary manslaughter without criminal malice, as our defense to mitigate murder based on provocation, then we have a chance to negotiate a lesser punishment. We still have a few days left to work on it and the public prosecutor, rather than drag this case out, may settle."

The attorney stood up and began pacing up and down in the little room, his lips quivering as he muttered to himself. He finally voiced, "Hmm. Yes. That's true, maybe." He continued, "But I would not recommend it. The court has appointed the judge for our case and I'm afraid it is not good news. This judge is an old coot, very harsh and not an admirer of foreigners on his land. He may take our plea of voluntary manslaughter as a weakness on our part and still go for the maximum sentence. No, no, I say we fight and remain firm on our original plea of not guilty. But it is your call, I can only advise you as your attorney."

"I agree with the attorney," David father chimed in without delay, "there is no way we are going to change your plea. We are not going to offer you as the sacrificial lamb because the police cannot find the real murderer. It is clear to me that the girl was strangled by her scarf and the person who stole both rare coins is the real murderer of both Antonio and Kitty. Case closed and this meeting is over."

David lowered his head in his hands. The sky was gray and sagging against the weight of innumerable skeins of rain. Outside a cool dampness infused the air—the sharpness of winter—and hung in misty gloom among the wintery branches of sleeping trees.

53

David had expected that. He was thankful for his dad's efforts—he knew his dad was only trying to do what he believed was best for his son—but David remained unconvinced. His dad had been absent most of his life, especially when he needed him, so he was certainly not in his debt. God Himself had been alarmingly absent in his complicated life, and he felt that he owed Him nothing either.

Quietly, as a man caught in a half-truth that he no longer cares to sustain, he admitted, "You know, Dad, you are right. One must fight for what one believes. I think that the new course I have chosen is in my best interests."

His dad's eyes narrowed and he voiced, "Is Maria part of this?" David could hear a tinge of hatred in his voice as he continued, "Did she put you up to this? Remember, it is her husband and sister we are talking about. How can you be so sure that she is on your side and not manipulating you to seek revenge? Italians are vengeful people."

He was staring at him, and when he caught David's gaze, he reached out and grabbed his arm. He insisted, "Does she really know how we feel, how you feel?"

David released his arm with a tug and in a firm tone responded, "She didn't ask me how I feel because she knows."

David's father, in an exasperated and yet pleading voice, pursued with, "You are young and your future is before you, but no one in the world can make his way unaided. Therefore, make use of your attorney's advice, its logic is sound, his good counsel will serve you for the rest of your life. And do not yield an inch of ground to that girl Maria; she will crush any hope that we may have. She cannot be trusted for she and her family are deeply involved."

"Before you say anymore," David said, "listen to me now, if only for the first, the last, the only time in your life."

"But son—"

"No buts, just listen," David continued with the persistence of a child. "I can give you my life, but not my convictions. The terrible monotony of my life is finally broken, to me all things are radiant with hope." He said after a pause, "I am not asking you to abandon me, you are family. I am asking you to support me. I am asking you to see my future from my point of view and what I want from my life."

David's father muttered inaudibly, whether in agreement or disagreement was unclear.

"You understood me," David said, looking back at him with unyielding eyes.

"A man who would give his life enthusiastically for a foreign woman and not be ready to die bravely for his own people and country is beyond my comprehension. But if this is what you want you will have no fight from me, be severe to none but yourself. Have it your way. But remember, for your own sake and safety, you are a soldier first. In your change of plea, think of it as taking the fight to them, but always be on your toes and make the first strike, draw the first blood. Be a proud soldier."

The attorney shook his head in disbelief at both David's decision and his father's speech. He gathered his files on the table and stuffed them into his black, leather briefcase and before departing, expressed that he had never lost a case in his entire career to date and would try to secure the best deal he could. But as a parting shot he again reminded David that the wild card was still the judge and warned him to use extreme caution when addressing the judge in his court.

David ignored the attorney's words and felt an icy sensation around his heart at his dad's words. Back on the war front, be a soldier again. Suddenly, David felt caught in a flash of clear, objective thought, on the churning sea of unthinking, tumultuous grief around him. So this is how history gets rewritten, he thought. This is how it begins, with exultation. Now it is not enough for a man merely to have been a man, now the etiquette of grief demands that we change him into a soldier, a hero. Now the flaws of a man have to be ironed out like wrinkles in a bed sheet, until he is spread out before the world as smooth and unblemished as the day he was born. He must be restored to his original glory—a soldier, a hero. In death, all men become saints, he thought, and he both welcomed and rebelled against the thought.

David, ignoring the severity of his attorney's warning, nodded casually. The day of darkness was near.

54

The night before David had to appear in court, he felt restless and barren of sleep. Maria's face when she came earlier today to wish him luck floated in his mind as he remembered how she'd thanked him. The damp cold draped itself like a heavy leaded curtain across the cell. For David, twilight was the loneliest time of the day. Darkness descended like fog rolling down a Tuscan mountain slope, engulfing the valley.

The night moved on imperceptibly. Unlike the day, it made no sound and gave no sign, but passed unseen, unfelt, over him till the moon was ready to step forth and appear through his tiny cell window. Then the eastern sky blanched, and the moon wrestled heroically to break free of the pack of clouds that hung on her like wolves on a white deer. As he looked at the moon he felt a sense of companionship. His own father, not understanding, had left him so alone that the solitary moon seemed nearer.

Precipitously the moon had escaped from the cloud-pack, and was radiant behind a fine veil embroidered with a lustrous halo, the largest halo David had ever seen. David stared at the light as myriad abstract thoughts flitted in and out of his mind. *I don't believe in a parallel universe but must admit that I live in the middle of two revolving worlds*, he thought. *The first is the idealistic but imaginary world, which we all yearn for. The second is the unreal world of unimaginable and unnecessary horrors that surround us. The middle, of course, is the real world, which is between the imaginary and unreal world and it is composed of the two. That is actually where I am.* As the night progressed, so did his abstract thoughts.

Suddenly he heard the rustling sound of a riot of leaves blowing across the courtyard below his cell window and he waited with bated breath in the stillness to hear them again. There was nothing but silence now. It's astonishing what you hear when you're alone. He closed his eyes, trying to visualize Maria's face again. A sound without shape or color is strange. To be blind is to hear otherwise.

As the night enfolded his body in its darkness he realized that her love, which he craved, was the light he must choose to live by. The might of obscurity is so strong that through the powers of night it successfully plunges the entire world into desolation, rendering all its inhabitants, human and animal kingdom alike, unable to do anything except to withdraw into an insentient state and surrender to unconscious sleep until dawn. Almost magically, at each and every dawn even the palest streak of eastern light accesses the very heart of darkness and begins to dissipate it with the prospect of life.

The light and warmth of the sun as it adorned the youth of day wiped out all traces of the night like it never existed. Celebrating the day with its bustling life everywhere like an invincible youth full of hope and ambition, often life ignores the dying light at dusk and seeks solace in the romance of the spectacular spectrum of colors of sunset. Inevitably the force of darkness overcomes the might of the sun and once again sinks the world into a still and lifeless state. All this amazing and incomprehensive display of nature just in one day on an unending cycle without cause and effect was happening without yielding its reasons why and David wondered if it would eventually end and take all its secrets with it.

David's thoughts shifted towards his father. He in a strange way liked his protests but he did not want him to go on like he did; he did not want to quibble with him. He could feel a new spirit inside, something strange and caring and slightly frightening. A part of David wanted to do what his dad was insisting on just to please him, but then there was new awakening in David that wanted him to grow up. And his soul was somewhere in tears, crying helplessly like an infant in the night. He wished his dad had not come. *He seemed to look at me, me, a failed soldier, a man of peace, for corroboration.* David liked the change and struggle towards the birth of a caring spirit in his father. But he still could not conform; his soul could not respond. If it was war, it was his war, his beliefs, and not his dad's, not anybody's but his. Nothing in the world is harder than speaking the truth, he decided, and nothing easier than flattery.

There are some questions that have no answer.

As he leaned against the cold wall he remembered the sunset when Mary had come to see him. Her golden hair was bright and shimmering and the sunlight had accentuated the depths of blue in her eyes. While they had talked of the future, especially where they would move for a new start in life, the setting winter sun like a bleached scepter was glorifying the barley fields, as if putting them into a deep slumber against the wrath of the onslaught of a harsh winter. David had given a long look to that sunset as if the glory of the west was bidding adieu to him, but he took solace in the fact that the light of the east was welcoming a new day in some far-off lands.

Unbeknownst to David, it was going to be a very cold and harsh winter followed by many others. A slip of moon waning in the sky reminded him of the fragility of life.

55

The falcate of hair, which like a Roman wreath fringed the back of his head, otherwise completely bald with blemished skull, ended at the furrowed ears in little tufts of steel gray mingled with fading black. His face bore a vague resemblance to that of a greying wolf with blood about its muzzle, for his nose was red and inflamed and gave signs of a life poisoned at its springs and cursed by diseases of long standing. His sloped forehead, too wide for the face beneath it, ended in a point, and, creased in kinked lines, gave signs of a life in the dark libraries, that of intense mental activity. It showed the burden of constant misfortunes, but extensive efforts made to surmount them. His cheekbones, which were brown and prominent amid the general pallor of his skin, showed a physical structure likely to ensure him a prolonged and lingering life. His hard, light-yellow eyes fell upon David like a ray of wintry sun, bright without warmth, anxious without thought, distrustful without conscious cause. His mouth was vehement and domineering, his chin long. He was the presiding judge and David's fate was at his mercy.

David thought that his attorney had not done him justice when he had warned him of the severity of this judge. The judge heard from the defense attorney the plea of voluntary manslaughter and contorted his face as if he had a bad taste in his mouth. The star witness Maria was examined and cross-examined severely but she remained firm and clear in her statement that reinforced the defense case of provocation and lack of criminal malice. To the utter horror of Affonso, the public prosecutor had accepted the manslaughter plea and in the light of first conviction, had asked the judge for a punishment of five to eight years with an early parole for good behavior. Obviously the defense attorney had fulfilled his end of the bargain and had produced the results he had promised to David and his father.

The judge heard many witnesses, and the closing arguments of both the public prosecutor and the defense attorney, and to everyone's utter amazement proclaimed that despite the explicitly established circumstances of provocation and lack of criminal malice, an example had to be set for people visiting the country not to trifle with local people's lives and families. He gave David ten years of hard labor with no possibility of an early parole.

David's attorney was aghast at this blatant decision, his father shouted curses at the judge and vowed to appeal the judgment and was eventually subdued by the police and removed from the court.

As David in handcuffs passed by Maria she whispered to him, "I'm so sorry, my love, but I will suffer more than you for I am the one to blame."

David expressed neither fear nor regret, but when Maria spoke to him, tenderness reappeared like a fire suddenly lighted. A prey to imperious justice, he gave no thought to the end of his journey for he knew that she would wait for him. In his defeat was a kind of triumph that only he understood.

A warm, noisy morning light was gathering over the city as the mist cleared, rising softly from the river. Fate, with wide wings, was hovering just over David. Fate, ashen grey and black, like a carrion crow, had him in its shadow. Yet David took no notice. The consciousness of having done his duty was perhaps his only reward, for he knew that the world of shadows filled with perpetual darkness has no gifts.

Maria, stepping out of the courtroom, looked at the day melting out of the sky, leaving behind the permanent structure of the night. The rosiness of the sunrise died hours ago as embers fade into thick ash. In her, too, the ruddy glow sank and went out. The earth was a cold dead heap, dreary in color, the sky was dark with flocculent grey ash, and she herself nothing but a column of an upright mass of grey ash. She knew a lot could happen in a decade and while his journey was about to begin, hers was at an end.

Book V
The Present
Winter 1993
Florence, Italy

56

The darkness gathered, draining the last of the daylight. In its increasing blackness it seemed as if the stillness of the room brought an ominous and inexorable message from the angel of death—it was judgment day. There were no stars out on this moonless night, making the blackness absolute. The silence in the room, instead of bringing calm, was saturnine. There was a peculiar sense of inevitability in the air. The priest felt that he ought to say something soothing to Mary, but she had either fallen into a shallow sleep, for her contorted face showed signs of anguish, or was just keeping still with her eyes closed, trying to build her resolve to face the preordained moment.

Suddenly Mary's body shook with a jolt and she raised her head from the pillow and looked around bewildered. She cried out, "Who's that? Who's that?" in a thick, gasping voice, turning her eyes in horror towards the window where the fern plant was swaying in the wind. With unnatural strength she had succeeded in propping herself up on her elbows.

The priest rose from his chair and held her frail and balled-up fists in his large hands and tried to calm her. "Mary, I'm here with you. You're in your house. You just had a bad dream."

Mary studied his face as if trying to remember who he was. Then her gaze settled on the fern plant on the window sill with its wet leaves swaying in the breeze and she started to breathe again. She was not dead yet, she thought. She let out a sigh of both relief and disquiet—relief for she had not yet completed her confession to seek redemption, and disquiet for the fern plant was there as a constant reminder of her tormented past.

She stared at him with swimming eyes and trembling lips, then turned her face to the wall. She wept silently. Padre could see her shoulders shaking, but could hear no sound. When she next spoke, she did so consciously. "My life has been a bad dream, Padre," she said in an almost inaudible voice as he slowly rested her head back on the pillow. "It will come to an end only when I go to my long sleep."

She focused on a large iron cross around his neck, half-protruding from the heavy folds of his robe. She wanted to touch it, but her arms did not have the strength to do so.

"You wear this cross," she narrowed her eyes, "with conviction or by tradition?"

The priest held the cross with one hand and with the other replaced the folds of his robe over it. "We all wear our crosses; some of us wear them inside and some outside. It is a symbol of justice. After all, God is just, and justice requires that wrongs be punished. The Bible recognizes the truth that all sin must be punished. My child," he said meditatively, "we have to obey His laws or be punished. And that is why God gave us a set of holy commandments. So, the cross is the place where Jesus paid the price for us, and in doing so, he united us to God."

"Father," she said, "tell me more about sins and punishment. What about sinners who go unpunished?"

"It is not for us to judge—"

He could not finish his sentence as Mary interjected, "What I mean, Father, is that if we mortals are compelled to punish sin, then do we become sinners when taking someone's life, if that was the just punishment?" She added, "What about a judge who hangs a sinner for his crime?"

The priest responded, "No, my child, for sometimes He delivers punishment through us. After all, we are a part of Him and our destinies are controlled through His guidance."

Mary simply nodded in relief, as if he had put a balm on her anguished soul. With moist eyes, she said, "Father, you now know my story. I had hoped the Madonna would shed tears of blood to absolve me from my sins and put an end to my sorrows. I have loved Her with all my heart, and prayed for her to weep for me and for all those who have suffered like me. So why won't she shed tears now that my time has come? Tell me, Padre, why won't she?" Her voice held a plea and she tried to lift her head. A spasmodic pain grasped her heart and squeezed it hard as if someone were wringing a wet towel with both hands. As an involuntary reaction she threw her head back and clinched her teeth to smother a cry.

"The cardinal rule of the universe is that everything is finite, so why is it that my ambitions have had no bounds? I wanted everything and was not afraid of the consequences. But I'm scared now, Padre, the shadows are everywhere. I think my time has come."

"You will be fine, try to get some rest."

"Oh, Padre, for years now, I've had nothing but rest and look where that got me. Nowhere," she said, breathing heavily. After a brief pause she asked, "'To open their eyes and turn them from darkness to light, and from the power of Satan to God, so that they may receive forgiveness of sins and a place among those who are sanctified by faith in me.' Isn't that what you once said? So, where is my light? Where is my forgiveness?" She cried as her body doubled up in excruciating pain.

The priest grasped her trembling shoulders to push her back into her bed. The sudden motion caused his cross to swing out of the folds of his robe and the sharp edge of it hit Mary on the bridge of her nose, making a cut across it. Her eyes closed and she went limp in the priest's arms. A rivulet of blood appeared on Mary's nose that drained into the corner of her eye. It appeared like a tiny tear of blood, as if through her Mary wept, making her last wish come true.

With the passing of her last breath her clinched fists opened. From each palm a pendant dropped on the hard marble floor, making a sharp sound, echoing in the large room. Both pendants rolled on their edges a few feet away from the bed towards the floor lamp and then came to rest. The air in the room was still and the room was silent. Under the gleam of the yellow-orange lamplight, the bright gold pendants took on a golden-reddish color, as if tainted with blood.

Mary's lifeless body lay on her bed with dried blood tears. She looked peaceful. The rain had stopped and the weather was calm outside. The fern on the windowsill was still and not a single leaf on its branches moved, as if the plant was holding its breath. In the distance a sudden shooting star lit the sky, its fast dissipating wake like magic dust, and then nothing was left but patchy darkness.

The full moon rose and with its gradual ascent, it relieved the world of darkness with its silvery light, bringing once again the promise of tranquility to tormented souls on earth. Northerly winds started to sweep down the Tuscan valley and gather strength as they swept through the city. A sudden gust in the street where Mary's house stood plucked the few remaining leaves on the trees, spinning them into an eerie frenzy.

The air smelled of rain, and in the perfect rectangle of moonlight cast by the picture window in the bedroom, Padre's eyes were on the lifeless and peaceful body of Mary bathed in silver. The rain started to fall and dance on wind gusts, as if offering the blessings of heaven. Mary loved the rain.

—The End—

Made in the USA
Charleston, SC
25 January 2013